DEADLY REUNION

ERNEST MORRIS

Good2Go Publishing

DEADLY REUNION
Written by Ernest Morris
Cover Design: Davida Baldwin
Typesetter: Mychea
ISBN: 9781947340053

Published 2017 by Good2Go Publishing
7311 W. Glass Lane • Laveen, AZ 85339
www.good2gopublishing.com
https://twitter.com/good2gobooks
G2G@good2gopublishing.com
www.facebook.com/good2gopublishing
www.instagram.com/good2gopublishing

ACKNOWLEDGEMENTS

First and foremost, I have to thank God once again for keeping me focused long enough to produce another novel.

Second, I would like to thank all my readers for supporting me and keeping me motivated to bring you into my world whether it be fiction or nonfiction.

A special shout-out goes to my homie EDWARD MOSES. Keep your head up, and be safe. Time heals all wounds, bro, and you're a fighter. Trust me, I know!

Shout out to my brothers: Kevin (Chubb) and Sedric (Walid) Morris. Rasheed, Frank, and Maurice Turner.

Thanks to Googd2Go Publishing for continuing to believe in me.

Shout out to Leneek, Nakisha, Brandi, Kendra, Meana, Le'Shea, Shayana, Sahmeer, Demina, Bo, Dee, Tysheeka, Tasha, Barry, Richard (RIP), Aliyah aka Fish (RIP), Queanna, Dwunna Theresa, Loveana, Ty, Peanut, Janell, Trina, Markida, Sharon, Aneatra, Phyllis, Eric, Andre, Eddie, Tamara, Janay, Bey, Yahnise, Nyia, Pamela, Symiya, Mira, Alisha, Shannon, Dee Dee, Damien, Nafeese, Kenya, Nyeemah, My Cheesecake Family, etc. Anyone else that I forgot to mention, it wasn't intentional, but thank you also. I've done it again!!!!

PROLOGUE

"Your Honor, on this very day of November 2, 2016, I hereby open this preliminary hearing by stating this cross-examination," the DA began his argument. "For the record, the defendant's counsel can save that statement or fact of evidence for the trial. Right now, the evidence I have on Mr. Jackson will prove without a doubt the degree of murder is first degree."

The DA paused for a second, then asked for permission to proceed. The defense attorney watched as he tried to make it seem like a show.

"Your Honor, may I proceed?" he asked, looking at the judge.

"Yes, Mr. Brown, proceed," he replied.

"Your Honor, the evidence against Mr. Jackson will prove to be first-degree murder."

"Objection, Your Honor, the prosecution is trying to go inside the mind of the jury, by painting a picture of the defendant as a murdering monster," Rique's attorney stated.

"Overruled," the judge said. "Mr. Smith, I'll

allow the district attorney to close up his opening argument."

"Thank you, Your Honor," the DA stated before continuing. "As I was stating, there's a stipulation between counsel for the purposes of this preliminary hearing. That stipulation is that on the date of November 8, 2008, James Washington, better known to the defendant as 'Champ,' was a human being. Furthermore, if called to testify, Dr. Craig Reed would testify that he is an assistant medical examiner for the city and county of Philadelphia, Pennsylvania. He will also testify that on or about the date of December 1, 2008, he had orders from his office to receive the remains of Mr. Washington after the body had been delivered from Temple University Hospital, where their victim had been pronounced dead. Dr. Craig Reed would testify that as a result of internal and external examination, the cause of death was a gunshot wound of fifty rounds from an AK-47, to the head and chest."

When the prosecutor finished his statement, the defense team was dumbfounded, but knew they still had a chance. Then he added, "He would testify that the manner of death was homicide."

I'm a, G about mine
I'm always holdin' a nine
These niggas crossin' the line
I'ma leave it right in his spine
I regulate on these herbs
I'm sickening with the words
I pitched on these curbs
I'm Iron Mike with the birds
Hold up
Donnie mathematical
Golden cross, sabbatical
Black hoodie, black panther
Huey Newton, I'm radical
Fuck around with them boys
I'm sittin' low in the Taurus
Diamonds on my wrist-piece
Fifty-something [?]
The Silverback of the Rap
In front or back of the track

And from the back of the trap, we forever clappin' the Mac
I done seen niggas get shot
I done bagged up in the spot
I done ran when it got hot
I done slept on that cot
Been gettin' money, imagine what I'm 'bout to do
You a bitch, name a hood that'll vouch for you
Get popped up, find yo ass chopped in two
Let's go!

—Styles P feat. Sheek Louch "Creep City"

Excuse my manners before going any deeper into the story of "Retaliation." It's only right that I take my readers back to the beginning where everything started at, so allow ya mind to relax and go on this journey wit me! Walk wit me . . .

CHAPTER
1

June 6, 2007

I'ma God in my hood, yea' good God

"SUPERMAN, GS UP, hoes down over here. Superman, Gs up, hoes down over here," Lil Bee kept screaming over and over, trying to move traffic in its proper direction.

"Ey, boy, let me get four!"

"Naw, young buck, she just hopped out that car over there. Ain't no way she's getting served before me. Fuck dat!"

"Damn, you ratting-ass old bitch, I'd hate to be ya co-defendant. How you out here looking a hot fucking mess, singing over some pills? Yeah, I jump straight in front of you! You see me. Bad bitches don't do lines, boo boo."

"Learn something, because if you knew better, you'd do better, bum bitch!"

“Yo, lil buddy, the little slick shit you popping ain’t necessary because bad bitches like X-pill. I ain’t seen one I couldn’t pop yet, so put some respect on old head. She the reason you little dusty bitches gotta lane, and as far as that line you ain’t trying to wait in, well you’re waiting today. This is a fucking hustler’s holiday, and ain’t no ass moving nothing around here, so how many you want old head?”

Bee turned his attention back toward the nice-looking brown-skinned old head chick.

“Two, young buck,” she said.

“Excuse you, bitch,” the young girl stated and rolled her eyes toward Bee and the old head chick.

“Listen, shorty, you ain’t gone keep disrespecting people, especially not out here on this block,” Bee stated to the ill-thick light-skinned chick, who now was ready to cause a major scene.

“Pussy, don’t make me call my brother. He’ll shut this lil nut-ass block down ASAP,” she replied.

“Bitch, I use to give a fuck, now I could care less . . .” Before Bee could finish his statement, Bay walked around the corner just in time.

"Keisha, I know you're not out here acting stupid telling people your gonna call your brother?"

"Why?" she said, getting smart.

"You know damn well that ain't gone happen. You gone get him hurt, baby girl. You better start thinking about others before you speak. Your mom still staying on Sigel Street, your grandma still staying on Broad Street, right? Your brother ain't built for this. You're gonna get his itty-bitty ass smashed with a sludge hammer. Now get what you came for and relax. Oh, and tell your brother I said get with me. I need that today."

"Bay, you ain't gotta get like that," Keisha replied. "That was uncalled for, and I apologize. Is my apology accepted?"

"Yeah!" Bay told her.

Before Keisha could turn and fully walk away, Bee yelled out, "Ey, Keisha, tell your crab-ass brother we 'round here eating hella lobsters. I thought that pussy was all you said he was. I see that shit switched up once Beezy came around. So, for now on, watch what you say to me, because I'm none to make a mountain out a mole hill, bitch."

Lil Bee and Bay, plus the old-head brown-skin chick burst into laughter. Keisha walked up Carlisle Street, talking on her phone with tears running down her face. She was so humiliated she forgot to even return to her girlfriend's car, who was now shaking her head from left to right not understanding why Bay would do her friend like that in public. At that very moment, the thought of giving Bay some pussy was now an afterthought! Him getting that type of satisfaction wasn't even worth the headache. It was clear he didn't give a fuck about anything other than them young bulls posted up on Carlisle Street.

As Felisha's thoughts ran through her head, she was suddenly interrupted by the sound of Clark Kent's brand new 645 BMW behind her, and at that very moment her pussy was moist from the thought of jumping on his pickle. She knew if she accomplished that goal she'd be looked at differently in the neighborhood. To be in the arms of a dope boy was every young girl's goal. They wanted to be the trap queen of the hood no matter what.

"It's young jizzle from the bottom of the map, gotta fifty round clip at the bottom of the strap, I do it for the trapperz wit the, the, the rocks, and them OG niggas wit the, the, the blocks."

As Byrd jumped out of Kent's 645, all that could be heard was the rasps from young Jeezy's voice. He shut the door and noticed the thick cloud in the air, and knew something wasn't right out there.

"Damn, young, wassup? You straight out this joint? Don't worry, our time's coming far as them big boy toys. You ain't gotta car watch that six like that." Byrd made a little light joke knowing his young bull far too well. Wasn't no car on his mind, it was something serious. "Come take a quick walk with me."

"Yo, I be right back," Bay stated to his young bull and headed toward Byrd.

"BM, this shit crazy, bro. Stacy's pregnant, lil Keisha just came through this joint tripping. I'm telling you now cousin I'm a fuck her brother over. I'm seventeen grand deep inside this block. I'm looking hard, but honestly I don't see my money coming back out this joint, bro. Seriously, this block gone drive me crazy, homie."

"Chill, young, you trust me, right?" Byrd asked. "Well listen, I'm a clean that little shit up as far as lil Keisha's brother is concerned. You go fall back with Stacy, and let the block run itself for a few days. Get ya mind right, and come back all da way up, bro. Oh yeah, here! This is twenty cents. That's the seventeen you're stressing over, plus three more. The middle man's really fucking the game up. I'm a change the forecast tonight, young. That's my word, bro."

"Alright, bro, scream at me once you touch back down or if my help is needed. That might be necessary, cousin. I might gotta air something out."

"Naw, baby boy. Just hit my jack if ever you're in trouble, dig me?"

"Say less! What's understood ain't gotta be explained, cousin," Bay replied. They shook hands, then Bay started walking toward Carlisle Street while Byrd jumped inside his rented Toyota Camry and pulled away from the curb.

In the next hundred block of Carlisle Street, Det.

Smart and his partner, Ross, watched as young people lined the block copping X-pills like a toddler going into a candy store. Fiends moonwalked frontward up the block, on the other side, as other junkies were trying to sell air conditioners. One fiend known as E-Mo tried selling one single Air Jordan.

"Smart, is your fucking eyes witnessing this shit here?" Det. Ross asked his partner.

"Yeah, I'm all eyes. These young limp dicks need some type of discipline. Look at them. His damn pants are around his ankles. The captain won't believe this shit. Take some more photos, partner. They're distributing that crap as if it were legal. That one right there is the kid Bee, right?" Det. Smart asked. "You really think he's gonna allow us to wire him up?"

"Yeah!" Ross stated, knowing all the evidence that was stacked up against lil Bee, plus he was holding an ace up his own sleeve. Sleeping with lil Bee's crackhead mother gave Ross access to Bee's room, where he found twenty bundles of crack, two loaded Glock-9mm handguns, and $3,700 of Bee's own money.

"Look, he's shoving his goddamn hand up that young girl's dress. Disrespectful sack of shit. She's around my daughter's age. Oh lord, I'm glad Reecey isn't built like that. I'd be doing overtime as far as this detective work," Det. Smart stated, shaking his head thinking about his own seventeen-year-old daughter.

Meanwhile, somewhere out in North Philadelphia

"10 bands, 50 bands, 100 bands," Drake played on the radio as Jeff sat stationed at the kitchen table, counting through the light forty thousand. He was double counting, triple counting it, making sure everything was straight as far as the paper was concerned. Honestly, he had no idea why Byrd wanted the paper so quick. He just knew something wasn't right, because they never played wit giving anyone this amount before. So, what was different about today? He didn't know yet, but he would soon find out.

Byrd was over at Neisha's house gift wrapping, stacks upon stacks of newspaper between hundred-dollar stacks of ones, fifty stacks total, making the grand total seem like it was supposed to be three hundred thousand even. After he was done wrapping the money, he left out and headed for his meeting.

~ ~ ~

Byrd sat parked inside Pathmark parking lot, right off Broad and Glenwood Avenue, waiting for the Ricans to pull up. Going over today's events and optical, the only thing that kept repeating inside his head was Bay's last statement and Jeff worrying about the move of him going alone. The thing that stuck out to him the most was those last words:

"MAN, YOU CAN'T TRUST THEM RICANS, BRO. THE ONLY THING BETTER THAN A CROSS IS THE DOUBLE CROSS. Let me go, Byrd."

Byrd shook his head free of the thoughts and watched as the Ricans pulled inside the parking lot right next to the Escalade he was driving. Byrd rolled the driver side window down and proceeded.

"Wassup, pop, you ready?"

"Si," Poppy replied, looking around nervously.

"Alright then," Byrd stated, tossing the bag into Poppy's lap.

He nervously looked through the bag, and on cue, Mary drove past Byrd's Escalade flashing her lights and hitting the sirens, and then kept moving through the lot. Poppy almost shit himself thinking about those twelve keys he had on-site as the patrol car drove past.

"Next time, pick a new location. Too many po po out here. Not safe for our business," Poppy stated nervously, pushing the large gym bag he retrieved from the backseat straight out the driver's side window.

Before Byrd could ask Poppy was he straight, the white Nissan Maxima was out of site and the black Dolce Gabbana gym bag was sitting on Byrd's lap containing the twelve fresh keys, for the price of $40k. Jeff had put together two thousand in ones, and three dollars' worth of cut up newspapers that were bought from the corner store.

"Damn, when you think shit sweet, shit gets sweeter," Byrd stated as he fingered through the keys, then pulled out of the parking lot slowly.

His hand was clutching his pistol as he looked around damn near 360 degrees. He was mouthing to himself, "I'm on that wave tonight, hope you niggas ain't try'na play tonight."

"Open up the pearly Gates, bright white lights Madonna. Angels lined up in my honor, ya' honor. Name me king, name me king. I took the crown, infiltrated their fortress. Kidnap the queen, rode away on white horses. Name me king, name me king."

~ ~ ~

It'd been two weeks, and Byrd had been laying too low. Shit'd been getting out of control. Taking shit lightly, lil Keisha's dick-head-ass brother slid through Carlisle Street, dropped thirty on Bay and Jeff, killed lil Bee, all head and neck work, shot five smokers, and tagged the old lady, Ms. Brown.

The very next day, the Puerto Ricans came back through looking for Byrd, just missing him by a few seconds. They were pissed off about being burnt, and they shot the block up, killing six people that were out there buying X-pills and critically wounding a few kids playing tag that couldn't leave the block. This news broke Byrd's heart knowing he was responsible for what took place.

"Damn, cousin, you sure it was the Ricans, bro?" he asked his man. "Alright, say less. I'ma cross path's wit them on a later date. Right now I gotta focus on touching base with Green. That little move he pulled don't sit well on my stomach, bro, real rap. Fuck he get that type heart from, knowing damn well his BM stays on Willie's block. I got that nigga though, that's my word," Byrd stated into his iPhone, before ending his call.

Byrd had the drop on Green as him and his baby mom came out the crib. He crept up on them, hitting Green twice in the back of the head. As his limp body hit the concrete, Byrd focused his attention on Green's screaming baby momma. He walked up to her, aimed the Glock 40 at her forehead then fired.

BOC! BOC!

CHAPTER 2

IT WAS THE fourth of July, and Custer Street was jumping. Everybody was out enjoying the first major holiday of the summer, and all the young bulls were out having fun. Shock just rode through, with thirty young bulls on dirt bikes and four-wheelers. They had big guns on their hips in plain sight as the air flicked their shirts up from popping wheelies. This Fourth couldn't go any smoother until now.

"Man, shake the fucking dice. You ain't gone keep sticking every fucking number. Fuck you think, this paper grow on trees? Niggas dying for less and living for more," Rique stated, growing frustrated. Him and a group of young hustlers were gambling craps on Custer Street.

"Rique, these peanuts. Fuck, you down ten thousand? I just brought my bitch that new Bentley GTC, cherry red for two hundred. Youngin' I could give a flying fuck about you getting frustrated over my shot. Stop what you don't like or you deserve to get stuck, you fucking young vick."

"Old head ain't gone be to many more 'vicks,' 'nuts,' or anything else that come out ya slick-ass mouth, I'm telling you now," Rique stated.

"Young nigga, you are and will be any fucking thing I say you are. Right now you my vick. Jazz needs Gucci bags and Chanel shoes, so pussy get daddy money, now eight dice, gator boots. That's it right there. Get my money, sucker," he shouted.

While Slim was on the ground talking slick, Rique was over his head making finger gun gestures for young Cain to go get the hammer off the car tire. Slim never saw Cain pass Rique the chrome .357 Magnum.

"Damn old head, I had enough for one day. I can't take no more. Please, man, stop the bleeding. Here go ya paper right here. I'm copping out."

"Damn, I knew you young niggas was sweet and soft, but I wasn't expecting big bad Rique to do no copping out, especially over some paper. But then again, sometimes you have to expect the unexpected."

That's exactly what happened as Slim looked up into the barrel of Rique's cannon, as he held it to the side of his head.

"Come on, young buck, not like this. That's Hustler Talk 101 in gambling," Slim stated, shitting bricks at the size of Rique's Magnum. You never would expect to see that look on Slim's face.

"Man, push that fucking paper back across and stop bitching."

"Alright, alright, chill, youngin'. It's all their money."

"Naw, this is all their money."

BOOM!

That single slug from the chrome .357 Magnum knocked Slim's brains right out of his head and all over his Jordan sneakers. Brain fragments were on Rique's face. Still in monster mode, once Slim's body collapsed to the ground, Rique stood over his body and fired away.

BOOM! BOOM! BOOM!

~ ~ ~

"Oh my God, Boo, this pussy yours. Yes, yes!

Please, I'm coming, don't stop, please don't stop."

That's all that could be heard throughout the apartment as Boo had Ebony bent over digging her back out from behind. She managed to get a few words in every so often, as she took quick breaks from sucking Bay's dick at the same time. This party train was in full effect. Only if Ebony knew there was a hidden camera sitting inside the corner taking still-frame photos to be sent upstate to T-Roy, who was cellies with her baby father.

Pictures speak a thousand words. The ones with her holding Boo's dick toward her mouth with one hand while spreading her ass cheeks apart with the other hand and Bay long dicking her brains out were going to make the Dream Team super sick.

"Put it in my ass, I'm cumming. Oh yes, right there," Ebony stated, before throwing her ass back rapidly, forcing Bay to stumble backward a bit.

Before Bay was fully able to regain control over the situation, he rammed every inch of dick inside Ebony's ass, as she shot a heavy load of cum all over his nuts.

“Shit,” he moaned.

She never missed one beat as far as keeping Boo’s dick warm inside her mouth. At that very second Boo shot his load, and Ebony was gratefully awaiting his arrival.

~ ~ ~

“Detective Ross, listen I’m nothing like my brother. Yeah, we was bonded by blood, but I ain’t cooperating on them bulls just to so-called help you build a case. Man, fuck that. You on your own. Do some detective work.”

“Reese, you gone help Detective Ross, or you getting the fuck out this house today.”

“Mom, you tripping. These the same people who paid for Bee’s funeral. These the same people who put food on our table, and now you wanna help this fucking jerk. Fuck that! I’ll take my chances out there, or die trying.”

“Baby, he’s gone give me two thousand dollars for this valuable information. Don’t you want them new Jordans?”

“Mom, you don’t get it! You really gotta stop

believing everything this fucking freak keeps telling you. He's hooked on cheap smoker pussy. Excuse my manners, but it's the truth. Even Stevie Wonder ain't that blind. Y'all both using each other, and my name won't be caught in the middle."

"Janet, your son is right. Let's not involve a child in our business. I'll handle things more professional from now on, youngster, okay?"

"Yeah, alright!"

~ ~ ~

"Will inmate FT-5573 Williams please report to the desk properly dressed? You have large mail. I repeat, FT-5573 Williams large mail pick up," the CO said over the loud speaker.

"Damn, celly, put that shit out and pass me that lotion real quick. I know she gone smell this cush all over. I just hope she don't try and book me."

"Yeah, Roy, just wait until later. Them joints ain't going nowhere. That's those pictures, right?" Dream Team asked, not even digging his baby mom was the main centerfold.

"Naw, bro, I gotta get them joints now, before

Deb wanna go through the mail extra hard on some tipping shit."

After T-Roy finished his statement and was properly dressed, he left out the cell and headed toward the front desk knowing once he returned and busted that United States Postal envelope open, Dream Team's mind would be forever changed, and he knew the relationship would be different in the cell. There wouldn't be any more talking about Ebony, the baddest chick down in Clear Field. Or how she wasn't fucking anybody and the pussy is only reserved for bosses.

The new conversation would be, "Damn, your folks out there treating my old bitch, but fuck her. I'ma do the same thing once I touch down." Having these types of thoughts made T-Roy skip down the tier a little faster.

~ ~ ~

Meanwhile, back in Philly

"When success take it's shot. What are you gonna do now? Are you gonna kill it? You gonna become unsuccessful? Frank, you can be successful and have enemies. Or be unsuccessful too and you can have friends. I got these niggas Breezy, don't worry about it. Let that bitch breathe . . ."

Jay Z's "Success" played through the cracked window as Boo stood outside the car wash on Broad and Huntingdon, waiting for them to put the finishing touches on his brand-new Yukon Denali truck. Boo was pacing back and forth talking heavy on his iPhone.

"Nigga, you must be super high, bro. It's World Gang running shit; ain't nothing else moving out here. I'm try'na tell you, soldier, you ain't ready for that type of drama. For one your reach ain't long enough, and your peeps damn sure ain't strong enough. Listen, bro, I really got the keys to the city. You niggas ain't on my level, so get your brakes tweaked first, bro, then come work out wit the boys. Man, you motherfuckers softer than lacrosse."

After making his last statement, Boo looked around before jumping into his Denali, ending the call, then turning right onto Broad Street, heading toward Cumberland Street. He was thinkingthat conversation didn't sit too well and the streets needed cleaning.

~ ~ ~

A few week later, Bay and Jeff sat quietly inside Bay's aunt's Ford F-150 pickup truck. His uncle Slim being murdered changed everything in the eyes of these two young hustlers. Everything wasn't fun and games anymore. Life wasn't all peaches and cream, and niggas were gonna have to choose sides after hearing the news, because in their eyes, retaliation was necessary. Rique couldn't and wouldn't get away with this murder as he'd done smoothly so many times before.

"Yo, I can't believe Slim gone, bro," Bay stated, breaking the silence. He and Jeff had been riding around for over two hours, with no main destination.

"I know, bro. Then it's super weird that it's Rique, bro. You could have never told me that he would move like that against the fam," Jeff stated, still in disbelief.

"Listen, bro, fuck that nigga! That's Byrd and

Boo's homie, not ours. He ain't no kin of mine, bro. He crossed the line point blank, and my folks are coming up from Atlanta today. I'm telling you, Jeff, these country niggas don't play games. My uncle has been telling me to bring them up for quite some time now. They kept saying that them niggas specialize in torture and murder. My cousin Buddy just walked off one of the nastiest homicides Atlanta ever seen, cousin. They're my uncle Slim's only two sons. They wanted answers from me, bro, and I'm going to point them in the right direction to draw first blood."

"Say less, bro! When do they touch down?"

"Tomorrow. It's just Buddy and Rambo. We gonna meet them at my aunt Pat's crib."

~ ~ ~

"Count time, count time! This is your 9:00 mandatory standing count. At the door with your light on. Commissary slips will be collected tonight," the CO announced over the loudspeaker.

"Damn, Roy, you've been reading that mail all day. What's up with them flicks Bay sent you? I know you ain't holding out on a nigga? That shit ain't for us," he said, standing up.

"Naw, never that. I just had so much shit on my mind them joints had me sick. I gotta get out there, but here," T-Roy passed Dream Team the pictures and walked toward the cell door.

He kept checking to see how long before the COs would be coming down the tier. Plus he wanted to be standing in case things got ugly once Dream Team ran across them flicks of his soon-to-be ex bitch. It depended on how lovestruck and pussy-whipped he was, but one thing was for sure, Roy knew the nigga's front game would be on a bean!

"Damn, Shock be fucking wit them bikes like this? I didn't know shorty was this nice, and yo, who this right here, cousin? Shorty super bad."

"Who?"

"Right here!"

"Oh, that's Kim from out West. The other chick, that's Pinky from Uptown."

"Damn, them niggas out there really having it their way. That's y'all folks, but they ain't fucking with me. Damn, that's Boo's Denali? Oh shit, Byrd got that new Escalade."

Dream Team floated through half the stack of pictures, and more hate and jealousy grew inside. There was no denying T-Roy's gang was out there winning. Private jets to Las Vegas, sky villa parties with super bad bitches, Bay hanging out the window of a Lamborghini in Miami. Jeff was right behind him, standing on top of a Rolls Royce Coupe. Then shit got dark.

"Yo, this Ebony, bro?"

"Where?"

"Right here, cousin! Man, I knew this nasty bitch wasn't no good. She out of pocket, bro. Ey, Roy, please don't show nobody these joints, bro. I'm surprise they let these joints through. This bitch out there getting partied, sucking and fucking on camera. She ain't got no respect for me or my son, bro. Seriously, if y'all wasn't folks, or I had another celly and these type joints came through—"

"Come on, bro, was that some type of threat toward the gang?"

"Naw, no threat! I'm just saying she outta

pocket."

"Pass them joints over. I'm ready to float through them joints again and scream at a few players over the jack."

"Naw, bro, seriously, it wasn't like that. It's no different than if your name was attached to a bitch and some flicks touch down in my direction. Dig me?"

"Yeah, say less. What's understood ain't gotta be explained," T-Roy stated, looking over the flicks again, with a grin on his face.

CHAPTER 3

THE NIGHT CAME and went, and it was a new day. Jeff and Bay were standing in front of two 6-foot-3, 260-pound animals. Buddy was the first to speak.

"Wassup, cuzzo? We gonna keep everything simple and light. What's up with the bull Rique, who is his team, and who's these niggas Tupp and D-Boy?"

Bay broke everything down leaving out no details. Rambo laid out two AK-47s, and Buddy pulled out the sweetest old fashion Tommy gun he had ever seen. After cruising around Philly for about two hours, Bay drove Rambo and Buddy through Custer Street, Clearfield, 32nd and Diamond, Arizona Street, to the Bad Lands, and through Hope Street. Bay wanted Rambo and Buddy to understand this wasn't Atlanta, this was Philly. It was necessary to understand what they were up against. After forty-five minutes of driving through different blocks, Bay pulled back through Custer Street, and sure enough, Rique's silver Maserati was pulling into a parking spot.

"Yo, that's that nigga's wheel right there," Bay stated excitedly.

Blood rushed through his body, knowing his mini tour around Philly had finally paid off.

"Box that nigga in, cuzzo," Rambo started yelling from the passenger seat while he gripped his AK-47 off the floor.

"Jam them," Buddy started yelling.

Bay shot straight into action leaving no space for the Maserati to move. Rambo rolled the passenger side window down, and Buddy rolled the back-passenger window down, and all hell broke loose.

BLOCA! BLOCA! BLOCA!

BOC! BOC! BOC!

Rique heard the sound of what seemed like a marching band going off on Custer Street, and shot straight into action. He thought that his young bulls were out there going ape shit on something and needed a little extra assistance. While Duck walked around Custer Street, Rique noticed that he wrong about his crew going crazy, and saw Bay driving with two people hanging out the window.

"Oh shit," he said, realizing the target.

BOC! BOC! BOC! BOC!

Rique's first two shots ripped through Buddy's shoulder. The next three shattered Bay's driver's-side window, missing his head by inches. The bullets found their mark in Rambo's chest, shoulders, and arm.

BOC! BOC! BOC! BOC! Rique's next four shots were all wild ones, landing into the bed of a speeding getaway truck.

"Damn, damn, damn," Bay yelled as he maneuvered the F-150 through traffic. He headed across Allegheny Avenue, then bust a hard left on Tioga Street.

Bay reached 9th Street in no time, found a secure parking spot, then helped Rambo and Buddy out of the truck. He ran down the only statement to say to the cops, then looked around making sure the coast was clear. He fired seven shots in the air, then dialed

911.

Later that night as Byrd lay in bed with Dakota channel surfing, the headline on Channel 6 News broke his train of thought.

"We're here live on the 3100 block of Custer Street, in the area of the city known as Badlands, where police were in pursuit of a Ford F-150 pickup truck in regard to a double homicide. The suspects got away before they could be apprehended. The victims' names are being withheld until their relatives have been notified. There are countless others with minor injuries, but they will make it. Officers found over two hundred rounds of shell casings on the scene from high powered weapons. Police have heightened patrols because of residents' concerns about the safety of their children. As we learn more information, we'll keep you updated. This is Jim McGhee, reporting live from Channel 6 News. Back to you, Melissa," the reporter stated.

"Damn, this lil nigga don't listen. I keep trying to tell him there's better fucking ways to handle that shit," Byrd stated, growing frustrated with Bay's tactics.

"Babe, you talking to me?" Dakota asked, still half asleep.

"Naw, something on the news caught my attention, that's all. Go back to sleep"

~ ~ ~

"Ms. Briggs, I'm Detective Single, and I would like to ask you several questions concerning the shooting death of your son Tyree Webster, also known as lil Bee, on Saturday, July 23, 2007. Can you tell me what information you have regarding his death?"

"Yes, on the day before Friday, July 22, 2007, somebody broke into Detective Ross's car outside my house. See, me and Detective Ross have been having an intimate relationship for the past few months," Janet stated, before continuing. "They used a dent puller and popped his trunk, then took about two or three guns. Ross left my house ramming, and kept saying he knew it was my son. The next day it had to be like 9:30 or 10:00 p.m. We were standing in the playground, and we heard all these gunshots.

About five seconds after the shooting stopped, Keen pulled up on his bike and said it was Detective Ross busting at Jeff and them. A couple seconds later Detective Ross pulled up on the scene wearing blue jeans, a black hoodie, and a black ski mask rolled up on his head. You could see the holes in the mask. I know he killed my baby."

Janet broke down crying on cue. It wasn't that she cared much about her son, it was more about Det. Ross finding out what she did and not coming around no more slinging that good dick and giving out free coke. She knew this was something that must be done if she wanted to earn the trust and love back from her son.

"Detective, I can't go back to my house. He'll kill me and my other son. It's not safe for us there anymore."

"Trust me, with this type of information I truly understand. We'll find you a witness protection program, but until then go back home and act normal."

"Okay, I'll try, sir!" After leaving 8th and Race,

Janet jumped inside the car with her son Reese and told him that it was done. “We got him, Son! I told you your mom was gonna make you proud one day.”

A few days later, Rambo and Buddy, had been released from Temple Hospital with just minor injuries. Luckily, Rambo’s bulletproof vest stopped the .45 slug from entering his chest. It still did its damage to both of their shoulder and arms, which were bandaged up identically like the Double Mint twins.

“I told you the niggas we dealing with are different type of animals. This ain’t Atlanta, so you can’t miss when dealing with these niggas,” Bay stated, pacing back and forth inside his aunt Pat’s living room.

“These ain’t your fucking average cats. These are fucking killers. Boo’s worth millions, Rique’s worth fucking millions, it’s levels to this shit. Y’all think coming down here with a few choppers will be enough? That ain’t shit,” Bay stated, pounding his hands together. “Man, y’all older, but this is my city. Start following my lead or get the fuck back on

Greyhound and go home."

~ ~ ~

A few miles away, a similar conversation was being held on City Line Avenue, inside a TGIF.

"Boo, what's up with the bull Bay? He's crazy coming through Custer Street with two niggas hanging out the window on some cowboy shit. Shorty picked the wrong fucking war, that's my word, bro. Boo, these niggas hit Monique sixty times, bro. My fucking son was inside his car seat, and she was pregnant with twins." He paused momentarily. Tears began to roll down Rique's face as he managed to finish explaining what happened. "Bro, my fucking twins' fetuses was hanging out of her stomach. I can't explain that shit to my son. Shorty gotta go!"

"Trust me, bro, you got my deepest condolences on your loss. I can't begin to image what's going through ya mind right now. I know for sure this is behind shorty feeling some type of way about his uncle Slim."

"Slim was shorty's uncle? He ain't learn nothing

from that? I don't tolerate disrespect, bro, on no level. I'm going to murder shorty."

"When, bro?"

"Tell Promo, it's fifty large on shorty and a hundred apiece on both of them other niggas. Matter of fact, fuck that! I'm a handle everything right after Monique's funeral. I'll shoot my son down to Atlanta, and after that, it's war time, bro."

The last two weeks had been hell. Bay had sent Buddy's and Rambo's scary asses back to Atlanta, and now it was only him, Jeff, and Shock causing hell on every block Rique owned. Bay shot up his barber shop, while Jeff and Shock firebombed Monique's mom's crib, killing Monique's lil sister Jasmine and their aunt Rasheeda. Jasmine tried her best to get out of the blaze by jumping out the second story window, only to find Shock standing there holding a M1 machine gun. He sent twenty rounds through her already burning body.

Now today was a special day because it was Monique's funeral. Rique had handled all of the arrangements, to make sure Monique was laid to rest properly. He flew in her cousins from Texas, her mother's sisters from North Carolina, and her father from the Dominic Republican.

Monique was dressed to impress, Versace shoes, a Chanel dress, and her gold diamond Audemars Piguet watch. Her casket was gold and white, and what seemed to be a million white roses surrounded her casket. As the service went on, every family member inside there had a moment, as the preacher performed a great service. You could hear babies crying, family members asking God, "Why her? She never hurt anybody." There were a few neighborhood chicks wondering where Rique was, and they thought he was wrong for not showing up. There were a lot of emotions pouring out of the church today, and yet the real show hadn't even started yet.

Bay, Jeff, Shock, and Bang Out sat outside Monique's funeral, listening to a State Property album, all dressed in black Dickies suits, ski masked down and strapped with an unlimited supply of heavy artillery. Bay was holding onto a MAC-90, sitting behind the driver's seat of the black Land Cruiser he had rented, while Jeff sat shotgun.

Shock and Bang Out just kept repeating, "We want, we want the niggas who shot that BB gun," both clutching twin Glock 40s with extended thirty-shot clips.

"Can they live, hell yeah, but they still gone die. We kill them, they kill us, we still got pride."

CHAPTER 4

"DAMN, SWEETY, YOU know I only ask for two things: love and loyalty. Trust me, I don't forget nothing. It's us against the world, baby girl," Byrd stated as his other line beeped. "Hold on real quick, my other line. Yo, what's up Bay? Yeah, alright get wit tonight. Hello, that was my youngin, but listen, back to us, check inside your dresser drawer. It's something special inside there for you, plus it's a note."

"Byrd what's this?"

"Just a little token of my appreciation."

"Oh my god, Byrd, thank you so much. You know you getting some pussy tonight," she said, looking at the Rolex.

"Naw, lil buddy, that ain't about no pussy. Is you following the instructions on the note?"

"Yes, I'm walking toward my walk-in closet now. OH MY FUCKING GOD, Byrd, what the hell is this?"

"Ha ha, little light Givenchy lambskin jacket. Get the note out the pocket, and do what it says, Sweety. What are you doing?" Byrd asked when it took her too long to respond.

"Following the instructions, bighead. I'm headed toward my shoe closet. OMG, babe, these the Louis Vuitton boots me and Candice saw the other day. She called you and told you I was crying about these ones, didn't she? Oh yeah, it's going down tonight. I'm a call and tell her we're having that threesome tonight. My baby deserves two bitches tonight, and your wish is our command."

"Oh yeah, multiple choices. It's time to pull the rose up, we getting ghost."

"Stop playing, Byrd! For real I'ma do it tonight."

"Alright, call me once both of y'all are ready," he said, ending the call.

RING, RING, RING!

"Yo, bro, what's up? You get them flicks?"

"Yeah, Bay, this nigga super sick, bro. Yo, the expression on that nigga's face was priceless."

"Ah, man, I'm trying to get these niggas prepared

and make them aware that these bitches out here ain't shit, dig me? Right now, I'm the one who's in control."

"Yeah that's another conversation for a different day. What's that other situation looking like, you got it under control?"

"Ah, man, when it rains, it pours. I move for real in these streets, bro. I'm really in a world with that piece. I'm like metal with that. Don't worry about that other shit, cousin. Just focus on exiting out that building. Until then, it's a purple heart for all them niggas. I'm straight out this joint, bro! Oh shit, I gotta meet Byrd. I damn near forgot. You need anything before I exit the building?"

"Naw, Jeff just sent me $2,500 last week. I'm straight. Just remember stay low and aim high."

"Got you, bro. With that lesson I'ma knock a few heads off."

"Yeah, that's what got me shitting bricks up in this joint." After T-Roy made that comment him and Bay both broke out laughing, because they both knew it was true.

"Alright, bro, I'm about to meet up wit this nigga Byrd. Get with me tomorrow, cousin."

~ ~ ~

Three hours later

RING! RING! RING!

"What's up, young?"

"Yo, I'm in traffic, trafficking. I'm serving birds and I'm serving herbs, so where we meeting before it's back to business, cousin?" Bay stated, talking slick.

"That's your problem. You smelling yourself too much."

"I sit back every day wondering where my baby boy went. You out this bitch going crazy. You and Jeff shot that girl funeral up for what? Fuck you gone get out of killing some pallbearers, then y'all firebombed her mom's crib. The nigga Rique ain't even around. He's laying low, until you're done, then he gonna strike. So what sense do it make for you to keep stacking up bodies and the nigga your searching for ain't around?"

"You right, cousin, but at the same time, once we out here making this type of statements, ain't no turning back, so fuck it," Bay stated.

"Damn, what happened to us getting rich, then looking back laughing at this shit?"

"We can still get there."

"You right, fuck it, guess it's my time. I gotta come down out of the coaches' box and play ball with you. Every time I'm trying to fade away, you keep calling me back."

"God damn, that goes without saying. I needed you, nigga. Mount up, and let's go."

"Young, you gotta understand these niggas super up. We ain't fully right to war with these type of motherfuckers yet. We got to fall back, build the bank roll up, then attack full throttle."

"Say less! What's understood ain't gotta be explained, my nigga," Bay stated, but he was smiling on the other end, knowing Byrd was now committed as far as going to war with Rique and Boo.

"Bay, you gotta be careful out this joint, real rap. Mary said the bitch Lynne Abraham emailed the 39th

District your picture, saying look into seven murders you committed. She got people showing up left and right making statements about this kid Bay from 15th Clearfield Street."

"Man, who the fuck is Lynne Abraham?"

"That's the head district attorney. If you gone be playing around, you gotta start knowing the main players," Byrd stated.

"Alright, say less! I'm a touch base with you tomorrow."

~ ~ ~

A few months had passed, and things were running smoothly. Jeff restored order on Carlisle Street, Bay was laying low down Ruby Street with Bricks. Byrd turned the twelve bricks he took from the Ricans into twenty. Things were almost back to normal until his phone rang.

RING! RING! RING!

"Yo, bro?"

"Man, you ain't gonna believe this shit, cousin. The whole time I was falling back listening to your advice thinking shit was running smooth, thinking these old niggas lost their steam, wondering why shit was running so smooth, questioning where the fuck these freaks been, these niggas been down in Atlanta making noise kicking up dust."

"What? Are you fucking serious?" he asked curiously. This was news to him.

"Yeah, this freak-ass nigga Rique caught my cousin Rambo coming out of Club Onyx strip joint. Boo already got Buddy, so they told Rambo if he does anything stupid, it's over for Buddy. Don't you know this country-ass dickhead throws these niggas his pistol. Man, my aunt Pat said once the club let out, Rambo was laying there on the curb with Buddy's head detached from his fucking body inside his fucking arms. This nigga done killed the dad and both sons, cousin. Man, they found Buddy's body on Peach Street, asshole naked with no fucking head on his shoulder."

"Damn!"

"Man, fuck that. I'm going down to Atlanta tomorrow."

"Them niggas ain't down there no more. They on

their way back up here. That's something I know for sure," Byrd stated.

"Well I'ma welcome their ass back home right at the fucking airport. It's about to go down in Southwest tonight."

"Be patient, young. This ain't the peewee league. We gone throw these niggas a surprise party for sure. I'm a get Mary to check the flight time of arrival, to see if them niggas departed from Atlanta and make sure they're coming back up here."

"See, that's why I needed Phil Jackson back on the floor with me," Bay stated, understanding in order to catch these niggas, Byrd was right, it had to be by total surprise.

~ ~ ~

Jeff had been floating around with the young chick Shana serving niggas all day. Him and his young bull Pistol.

"Ey, Jeff, my folk wants two and a quarter. You gone serve them and let me make a few extra pennies since y'all been burning my gas out all day?" Shana asked.

"Yeah, that ain't about nothing. Where they at?"

"Down Atlantic Street."

"Where the fuck is that at?"

"Down Frankfort Avenue."

They turned on Atlantic Avenue, and Shana pulled over in front of the crowd of young bulls, looking for her cousin Rock.

"Y'all seen Rock out here?" she asked them.

"Yeah," one of the young niggas stated from the crowd, looking into the car trying to figure out who was all inside.

"Baby Frog, stop fucking looking like that. It's me, Shana."

"Oh shit, yeah, Shana, he inside the crib waiting on you. Get out the car, stop acting crazy with that big ole ass. When you gone let me fuck Ms. Parker?"

"Boy, ya lil ass can't handle this ass," Shana stated, getting out the car with lil Pistol right on her heel.

Jeff stayed inside the car talking on the phone busting other traps. As Shana and Pistol made their way through the front door, to Pistol's surprise, there wasn't anybody there buying coke. The only thing inside the living room was a metal chair with handcuffs around the arms and legs.

"Shana, what the fuck is . . . ?"

Before lil Pistol could finish his statement, Rique slapped him over the head with a brand-new Colt 45 handgun, splitting him straight down to the white meat. Outside, Jeff caught the action out of the corner of his eye and slid over into the driver's seat and pulled out of the parking spot slowly. Once he made it to the corner of Atlantic Street, Jeff pulled over, pounding his hand on the steering wheel. He checked the rearview mirror, making sure he didn't draw any attention as he pulled out of the parking spot.

Back inside the crib, Rique successfully placed lil Pistol on the metal chair, strapped both sets of handcuffs around his arm and legs, then told Shana to go outside and tell Jeff her cousin Rock wanted to holla at him. Once Shana opened the door, she noticed her car was gone.

"He's not out there!"

"Fuck you mean he's not out there?" Before

Shana could repeat herself, the first shot rang out.

BOC!

Jeff came back down the block military duck walking, firing toward the crowd. If lil Pistol was going out, he wouldn't be the only one.

BOC! BOC! BOC! BOC! BOC!

Jeff's first two shots ripped through Baby Frog's face, knocking his Phillies hat two feet into the air.

BOC! BOC! BOC!

The rest of the crowd took off running in different directions. Rique's main young bull, Sean, gripped a MAC-11 and started squeezing off all sixty shots by finger fucking the lemon trigger.

BLACCCC! BLACCC! BLACCC! BLACCCC! BLACCC!

Jeff returned fire, backpedaling, trying to get the fuck out of the way as Rique's MAC shattered every car window on Atlantic Street.

"Damn it," Jeff yelled out, jumping into Shana wheel and pulling off.

He quickly turned the corner, then headed toward Allegheny Avenue. As soon as he made the left turn, he noticed the blood running down his shoulder and felt the pressure of pain going through his back. At that very moment, Jeff passed out, crashing into the bank on the corner of Allegheny Avenue.

CHAPTER 5

Inside Temple University Hospital

"YO, WHAT THE fuck is going on, and why am I handcuffed to this fucking bed? Get these things the fuck off of me," Jeff snapped.

"Sir, you gotta relax, okay? You've been shot, and crashed into the bank on Allegheny Avenue. You're handcuffed to the bed because the officers wanted to talk with you once you were awake. Your family members have already been here. To my understanding you're a well-loved man. Here," the nurse said.

"What the fuck is that?" Jeff asked.

"That's a handcuff key. Your brother gave me $10,000 not to report your blood work, so the police won't know who you are, and another $10,000 to give you this handcuff key. My job here is done. That's the door right there. That will lead you into another room. There's another change of clothing inside the closet. Your sister Mary will be waiting for you outside in her squad car."

"Thank you very much! I appreciate this, Doctor."

"No name," Candice replied with a slight smirk on her face.

There wasn't really anything in this world she wouldn't do for Byrd. The only problem she had right now was that sharing him with Sweety was starting to become old news. Soon things would change in her mind.

Back on Atlantic Street, the police still had the block taped off. The news reporters left, and there was only one police car still there guarding the scene, finishing up the paperwork. Rique was inside the house, peeking out the window. Right behind him was now a naked Pistol, still strapped to the chair. He had a washcloth over his face, and Rique's Gucci belt was strapped around his forehead, stretching his head backward. Rique returned from the window and picked up a fresh gallon of water off the floor. He removed the seal from the top, and proceeded to pour water over Pistol's face until he heard that choking for air sound, then stopped.

"Pussy, you gonna talk now?"

"Man, I'm . . . I'm telling you, I really don't know them niggas like that," Pistol stuttered in between, trying to regain control over his breathing.

"Oh, you just a young neighborhood dick eater. Well you know what happens to dick riders, right?" Rique stated, then walked toward the kitchen, heading down to the basement. A few seconds later, he returned holding a blowtorch, some salt, and a big-ass kitchen knife.

"You dumb young niggas don't respect no rules. Why y'all keep playing with me?" Rique asked, lighting the blowtorch up. With one swift motion Rique place the lit torch on Pistol's cheek and burned a hole right through his face.

"Owwww, shiiiit, I swear, I swear, please man. Only thing I know is Byrd riding with them now, that's it," Pistol stated. He was spitting blood out of his mouth, and two teeth fell through the hole of melted skin.

"Nigga, I didn't ask you shit about Byrd, but I'm glad to know you're willing and able to give up some info," Rique stated, and proceeded to cut his kneecaps with the large butcher knife. Next, he chopped two fingers off Pistol's left hand.

"Oh God, please, man, just fucking kill me, please." Pistol's request fell on deaf ears as Rique stuck the knife into his eye and removed his eyeball right out of its socket. He used the torch to burn his eye socket shut.

"Pussy, stop fucking crying like a bitch," Rique stated, then threw salt onto all his wounds.

"Man, just kill me," Pistol said again in a low, soft, painfilled whisper.

"Man, just kill me, please," Rique teased him. "Naw, nigga, life ain't fair like that. You gotta go through some shit and come out a fucking legend. Then you die and let your story be told. I'ma take your little soft ass through some legendary torture shit and let the streets talk about this shit later." Rique fumbled through his pants pocket and retrieved his cell phone, then started taking some photos of Pistol. “Nigga, you really wanna die?”

Without waiting for an answer, Rique turned the blowtorch up higher and stuck the nozzle through Pistol’s cheek, leaving it there until his whole head started to catch on fire.

~ ~ ~

“Gang, y’all ain’t heard that in a minute, huh I said I wasn’t gone do no more four minutes of hell man, this gotta be it, this the last one. I’m from the jungle lies, apes and gorilla, lies the police, nigga we the apes and gorilla, boy don’t turn ya face on a killer, fuck the system we going back to racism nigga . . .”

“Yo, cousin, turn it down real quick. This’s the call I been waiting on,” Bay stated. Him and Shock had been riding around listen to Lil Herb’s “4 Minutes of Hell.” “Yo, Mary!”

“I successfully got your hot-ass man Jeff out the hospital.”

“Alright, drop him off at Shar’s crib. Oh, and did you get that information on the bitch Shana for me?”

“Yeah, it’s, 3188 N. Jusup St. Apartment A1, second floor.”

“Alright, I’m on shorty’s ass tonight. Don’t tell Byrd!”

“Boy, I’m a cop, but I ain’t no cop,” she reminded him.

“Sorry, M, I almost forgot who I’m talking to,” he replied, smiling.

“Yeah, don’t forget that I raised your lil bad ass, and I’m trying keep you out of prison at the same time.”

“I appreciate that, baby girl. You know you the first lady behind this World Gang shit.”

“Bye, boy!”

“Alright, talk to you later,” he said, ending the call.

~ ~ ~

RING! RING! RING!

“Detective Ross, 39th District.”

“Ross this is Detective Single, down at homicide. Before going any deeper into this conversation, is this a secure line?”

“Yeah, speak freely, this is my personal line. It’s airtight!”

"Okay, well I'm one of the lead detectives who oversees cases down inside your district. A few days ago, I had a woman by the name of Janet Briggs come into headquarters."

"Why?"

"Let me finish. Anyway, she came into headquarters, speaking freely about her son's murder. It was valuable information until she stated you're the one who committed the homicide. I looked out my office window as I was going over the statement she made, and witnessed her and another young man hugging. I thought to myself that was strange being that not even a few minutes ago, she was just in full tears, crying you were behind the killing. She also stated something about you having a sexual relationship with her. Now, Detective, from one detective to another, your house is very messy and could use some spring cleaning, and fast, before these same waves cross over into something major."

"Detective, this trash will be taken care of tonight, but honestly, what do I owe for this act of kindness?"

“Well, a very good friend of mine need a favor, and he’ll personally handle your mess for you, because it’s more like killing two birds with one stone.”

“Okay, I’m all ears!”

“Well, see, we need you to arrest this Bay character. Bring him to a stash house up in Frankford on Penn Street. I’ll text you the address once you have him. Is that a deal?” Det. Single asked.

“That’s not a problem. When can I expect my situation handled, because even with Janet lying, if that lie reaches the wrong hands my career will be finished in this town.”

“Well, that major white lie will be lying six-feet deep by tonight. That’s my word.”

“Okay, cool! I appreciate the act . . .” Before Det. Ross could finish his statement, the line went dead and Det. Single looked toward Rique and smiled.

“You’re only ten steps ahead because of me. Now you can get out of my vehicle and start today’s mission.”

CHAPTER 6

"FIVE, FOUR, THREE, TWO, ONE, HAPPY FUCKING NEW YEAR!"

Bay and Byrd stood side by side in the middle of Times Square, surrounded by millions of people gathering around hugging and kissing, enjoying bringing the New Year in with their loved ones. Byrd was dressed down wearing a double buttoned Burberry military coat, True Religion jeans, and Louis Vuitton sneakers, while clutching a thirty-shot Glock 40 tightly. Bay stood next to him, dressed down in a Chanel flight jacket, Seven jeans and Dolce & Gabbana boots, holding a sixty-shot MAC-11 tightly.

"Byrd, this nigga Boo can't be serious, bro. After all this, he's in Times Square hugged up with some bitch. Come on, it's now or never," Bay stated, slowly inching through the crowd.

"Naw, not yet, Young!"

Bay never heard Byrd and kept moving toward

the crowd. At that very moment, Boo heard someone say, "Watch out," and turned around to Bay holding a sixty-shot MAC-11 over a screaming white girl's shoulders, and squeezed.

BLACCC! BLACCC! BLACCCC!

Within that very difficult moment of Bay not having the proper angle, Boo maneuvered Star into position directly in front of him and swiftly pulled his own Glock 27 from underneath his Prada jacket and fired off wildly.

BOC! BOC! BOC!

Boo's first shots silenced the white girl's screaming at point blank range. The bullets ripped through her forehead, exiting out the back, sending brain fragments directly over a little boy's face, who watched from his father's shoulders. All that could be heard throughout Times Square was loud fireworks, gunfire, police bull horns screaming, and police horses fighting to get loose from all the pandemonium.

"Young!" Byrd yelled, seeing the New York police officers moving through the crowd. He did what came natural and let off seven rounds in their direction to give Bay enough time to duck through the crowd and get low.

~ ~ ~

Meanwhile back in Philly

Shock was inside the bar on 30th and Styles, enjoying a little light conversation with Shana while watching the ball drop on TV.

"Damn, so where you really from?"

"Really, I'm from Diamond Street, but I be hanging down North with my cousins. Why, you the police, asking all these detective questions?" she asked suspiciously.

"Naw, I'm too real for cop or detective work. I'm just trying to make sure we ain't already running inside the same circles. Less drama, dig me? But listen, this bar scene ain't really my thing. We already seen the ball drop. What's next?" Shock stated.

"You tell me."

"Come on, we out!" Shana followed Shock's

lead, thinking something sweet was hook, line, and sinker, not knowing what the night had in store.

~ ~ ~*

"Mary, why keep waiting around risking your career, knowing damn well you are deeply in love with this man? You gotta sit him down and explain the circumstances and situation at hand. Tell him how you feel. Let him know that you're out here risking your freedom and life to make sure he's alive when you wake up. I spend many nights without any sleep, worrying sick about your well-being. Tell him everything you tell me at night, and if he don't respect that, then he ain't the one for you," Ashley stated.

"Ash, you really don't understand. I've been chasing behind Byrd since we were fourteen years old. He's my everything, and what's crazy is, he knows I ain't going nowhere. I mean he comes home to me every night, but I know deep down he's fucking other bitches. I'm afraid him and Bay are gonna get killed out there, or go to prison for a very long time. My heart can't take it if something happens to them out there in those streets."

"Listen, girl, my Dominican friend is coming up from Texas. In order for us to survive, Byrd, Bay, and the rest of their team have to be on the same status as Rique and Boo."

"We're gonna rob them niggas."

"Girl, I never did no shit like that before. Byrd only allowed me to ride past and flash my lights, that's all."

"Well today is different. We're doing more than riding past flashing some damn lights. We're takin' paper and work today, and it's gonna be smoother then a baby's ass. Watch, he's gonna be super proud once we touch back down with this bag," Ashley stated.

~ ~ ~

Over on 11th and Indiana, Jeff had just finished digging up a super-sized hole in the pet cemetery. He was finishing up with shoveling the dirt to the side, when Shock's car was pulling into the gate. On this New Year's night, the weather was perfectly nice, with foggy conditions, and a heavy mist. Shock jumped out of the driver's seat and walked straight to the trunk and opened it up. There lay Shana, confused, shocked, and fearing for her life. Shock removed the duct tape from over her mouth to ask her a question.

"Do you recognize my bro?"

"Jeff, please, Rique made me do that shit. I swear I wasn't gonna cross you. That's why Pistol came inside the crib."

"Well tell Pistol that, because I'm still breathing, baby girl. See, y'all played a nasty little torture game with a good young nigga. That shit hurt my heart every day, knowing I didn't kill you or that fuck nigga Rique, but you see how life goes. You do dirt, you get dirt!"

With that being said, Jeff grabbed Shana's arms while Shock grabbed her legs. They both carried her shaking body to the open hole and tossed her in.

"Jeff, this shit ain't funny. Please, I got kids. Help me out of here," Shana called out to them.

Her cries fell on deaf ears, because Jeff and Shock began to throw large amounts of dirt on her body. Shock went to the car and returned with a duffle bag full of rats. He opened up the bag and tossed it into the hole. Shana damn near lost her mind as rats ran all across her body.

“Even when the sun goes down, we gone make this motherfucker light up,” Jeff stated, pouring gasoline inside the hole all over Shana’s body.

He reached into his pocket, removing a book of matches. Shana started screaming when she smelled the gas, but they paid her no attention. Jeff tossed the lit match into the hole, causing it to erupt in flames. They both laughed as they watched her screaming body burn to a crisp.

CHAPTER 7

"YEAH, HOCKEY RAW, that's a good situation over on your side, bro. What's the name as far as the block?"

"Warnock and Huntingdon," Hoc stated.

"Alright, me and my homie is driving back from New York right now. Once we reach Philly, I'ma hit your jack and let you know if everything's a go. More than likely it's on, bro. We gotta switch fields anyway, so green light everything. It's on, fuck it."

"Alright, Byrd, say less."

On Roosevelt Boulevard, inside the cheap Day's Inn, Ashley entered the room with Jazz, her player from Texas. They got straight to the point without wasting any time. She started by removing his clothes, then blindfolding him. Next she put her own police-issued handcuff on him, then read him his Miranda rights.

"You have the right to remain silent. Anything you do and say will be held against you in a court of law." Once the handcuffs were successfully around Jazz's wrists, Ashley got up and went to the door to let Mary in.

Mary walked straight over to Jazz and removed his blindfold.

"Jazz, I bet when you woke up this morning you didn't think your silly ass would be getting cuffed and robbed by two female officers. Listen up clearly, nigga, don't you ever come around here anymore with your country ass," Mary stated.

She headed over toward the bathroom and opened the door. She found two large duffle bags lying inside the tub, which she grabbed, heart pumping with fear, excitement, and nervousness because she knew Byrd would be rich now. She was going to get an ear full once she explained what she had done.

"Here goes nothing," Mary stated, and walked out the door, lugging both bags down the stairs and straight to the trunk of her Camaro. Seconds later, Ashley came walking out of the hotel smiling from ear to ear.

"See, bitch, I told you it was gonna be easy and sweet."

"It was easy," Mary said as her adrenaline calmed.

"Now we take this to Byrd and see if he likes what's inside," she said as they left the motel feeling good about what they had just accomplished.

~ ~ ~

Cruising across the Walt Whitman Bridge, Byrd and Bay had the music down low, as they were deep in conversation.

"Damn, young, we've been at this shit for months, cousin, and almost lost you today. You know the type of fear that shot through my body, bro? All I saw was flashes and flashbacks of me telling you shit was gone get greater later. Those late-night rides down South Philly to eat at Geno's Steaks, getting that first phone call after you hit that lick with Papers, and that first shootout I took you on. Man, honestly, I regret exposing you to this life, because at the end of the day, I know one of these days I'm going inside the ground or behind them prison walls. Real rap, I can't take you on that type ride, bro."

"Byrd, what's our motto, 'World Gang or nothing,' right? Well listen, I'm built for this, bro. I'ma get this money, live life, fuck these bitches, and make them remember I was here and put it down how real ones do, bro. Remember that first lick me, you, and Boo was supposed to hit and I came back to the wheel crying because you wanted me to kill old head? You kept saying we already got the work, hit him and keep it pushing. Ever since that day, I promised myself that I'd never let you or myself down again," Bay stated.

"Young, don't never think you ever let me down. We gang and I'll go to hell and back for you. I'm with you and never against you, no matter who we up against; fuck them, bro. Listen, you staying with me tonight. We'll get with everybody else tomorrow morning. We gone change everything up, start fresh; it's a new fucking year. We brought it in super fresh, big bank rolls and loud .44s, so we gonna end it off with more money and more gun smoke. When you hit a lick, you control the scene, bro."

"I feel what you saying, hit a major lick, and it's about takin' blocks, then networking for more blocks."

"That's right!"

RING! RING! RING!

"Yo, M, what's up? . . . Alright, I'm bringing Bay with me . . . Yeah, I had his lil crazy ass with me all day . . . I know, you love both of us. Have you been drinking? . . . Alright, I be right there . . . Naw we was over New York," he said, talking to the caller. He put his phone on speaker. "We were just watching the ball drop."

"Byrd, I really, really love you," Mary stated, getting emotional as she stared down at the neatly wrapped fifty kilos of cocaine and the $375,000 in cash.

"M, I love you, and I've been in love with you since we were kids. You gonna marry me?"

"Byrd, stop playing, what did you just say?"

"M, you're not crazy or slow. You heard me right. Now, is it yes or no?"

"Yes, yes, yes! How far away from home are you, because I got something special for you and Bay?"

"Damn, I'm the one who proposed. How come Bay gets some action?" he joked.

"Byrd, stop playing so much. You know damn well Bay's little bad ass ain't getting none of this cookie," she shot back. "I raised him, but there's somebody here for him."

"Alright, we about five minutes from you."

"Yo, you really gonna marry, M? Real rap, cousin, don't play with her heart because she might be the one who kills both of us. Her good cop shooting ass," Bay said laughing.

"Naw, I'm really gonna marry her, bro. We starting fresh with everything. This is our year, bro, I feel it."

"I can feel it in the air tonight, hold on."

Both Bay and Byrd broke out laughing after Bay stopped singing Phil Collins's hit song. They both jumped out of the car in front of Mary's house, still singing.

"I can feel it in the air tonight, hold on."

Mary opened the door smiling. Then her expression changed once she saw the blood all over Bay's and Byrd's clothing.

"Get in here! Look at y'all's fucking clothes," M said.

Both Byrd and Bay looked down and noticed how much they was slipping. They realized that they drove from New York back to Philly covered in a major crime scene. They just shook their heads and walked in Mary's crib not saying one word.

"Listen, Byrd, promise you won't get mad or snap out about everything I'm about to tell you and show you?"

"Listen, M, I already had one of the most weirdest days ever. If it's something crazy or stupid keep it to yourself. Let that be last year's little secret."

"Byrd," Mary stated, starting to cry.

"Listen, I don't want you and Bay going to war not having the same type of money or supplies as these niggas out here. I know you said I better not ever put myself in harm's way as far as my job, and to only focus on doing my eight and skate. Well fuck that, if y'all all in, so is me and Ashley."

"M, what the fuck is you talking about? So, is you and Ashley? You and Ashley what?" he said aggressively.

"This," Mary stated. On cue, Ashley came out of the kitchen carrying the two large duffle bags. She opened them both up and showed them the contents. "That is fifty kilos of pure cocaine, and this is $375,000. Me and Ashley are takin' one hundred thousand a piece, and you and Bay are gonna do y'all with the fifty keys and the other $175,000."

"Only under one condition," Ashley said. "Bay gotta be mines and only mines."

"Listen, Ashley, I appreciate everything you saying and doing, but I'm telling you now, my BM coming with me. There's no way I'm leaving her for no amount of paper or out in these streets without me. So, if you agree upon that, it's on."

"Promise you'll always protect me the same as your child's mother?"

"Ash, won't shit be different, I promise you that

much," he stated boldly.

"M, don't let their little love moment and conversation think you're off the hook. Go 'head, Ashley, you and Bay separate everything how y'all said. You, Ms. Billy the Stickup Kid, upstairs so we can talk."

"See you in the a.m., Ash. I knew this was coming. Come on, dad," Mary stated, rolling her eyes at Byrd and bouncing every inch of her five-foot-two-inch frame up the stairs.

"Ey, Bay, I could feel it in the air tonight, hold on." The four of them broke out laughing.

~ ~ ~

"Damn, I swear, cuz, I ain't know shorty was that type bitch. She helped me move hundreds of keys, cuz. I promise I'm a get your paper back. You ain't gotta worry about the loss, that's on me. I accept full responsibility over the load, and I'll replace every dime. Cuz, I ain't leaving this city until shorty's stinking some fucking where. This bitch had the nerve to handcuff me, blindfold me, got me thinking it was going down. I'm a kill shorty, cuz."

"Listen, Jazz, I really don't give a fuck about your sad-ass story. Don't come back down Texas without my money. Better yet, don't come back at all. Tonight, I'm killing your mother, your sister, your wife, and those two little boys you love so much. They're all good as dead, I swear. When you reach Texas, you'll smell the burnt skin, hair, teeth, every fucking thing you remember and love about them. It will all be up in smoke, I promise. Mark my words, nigga."

Click! Dame ended the call without giving Jazz any chance to respond.

CHAPTER

8

RING! RING!

"What's up, Dame? To what do I owe the honor of this call?"

"Ah, bro, stop that. Listen, Rique, I ran into a little situation down in your neck of the woods. I sent my stupid-ass driver down to Philly to handle a little light load. This stupid nigga picked some chicks up and they ripped the whole load. My guess is, it was some regular young chicks that ain't really into the streets. They seen a vick and took advantage of the situation."

"What's the chicks' names?"

"I ain't really sure which one, but one of their names is Ashley. Supposedly they're both cops."

"Alright, give me twenty-four hours and I'll hit your jack back," he stated, ending the call.

Around 12:30 p.m. the very next day, Boo sat bandaged up inside his condo outside of Camden, New Jersey, talking on the phone with Tupp. He was watching the *First Take* sports show on ESPN 2.

"Cousin, I'm telling you, Byrd ain't the same nigga, bro. These two niggas tried to earth me. Then it's crazy because it wasn't no coincidence, like we both just so happened to be in Times Square. Man, the bitch Star lined that one up, bro." The other line beeped as they were talking. "Hold on, cousin, the other line. Yo, what's up, Rique?"

"Yo, you ever heard of this bitch named Ashley before? Supposedly she a cop."

"Yeah! If it's the same Ashley I'm thinking about, she works for the 39th District. Shorty good friends with Byrd's bitch Mary. Oh yeah, speaking of these niggas, they had me last night, but listen, I'm on the other line with Tupp. Get with me at the spot around two o'clock."

"Alright, bro!"

"Yo, Tupp," Boo said, clicking back over. "My fault, bro, but yeah, anyway, the little bitch tried some hoodwink shit. I ended up using the bitch as a human shield. Bay hit her ass up twenty times with that MAC. Her little frail body twitched and bounced all over. Them fucking slugs went right through the bitch, fucking my vest up."

"You lucky, bro, real rap, shorty out here running and gunning something like coach K," Tupp stated.

"Well this ain't Duke, bro. I'm on his little ass now, and I'ma handle mines.

~ ~ ~

Back in Philly, a different conversation was taking place. All sitting around a large round table mafia style were Byrd, Bay, Jeff, Shock, Fatman, Mary, and Ashley. Byrd had the floor, and everybody's full attention was on him.

"Listen, without going into full details, Mary and Ashley did some shit that's gone change the game forever for us," he began. "From now on, Shock, your job is to protect them. Their job is to work and find information on cribs worth hitting. Shock, you and Fatman gonna handle that. Jeff, your job is to murder anything they need murdered as far as those jobs or inside these streets. Plus, you will control Carlisle and Mayfield Street. Me and Bay are going to the other side, on Warnock and Huntingdon, with my man Hoc."

Everyone nodded in agreement, supporting his decision. Byrd continued with the meeting for another hour, going over in more explicit details the roles everyone would be playing. When he was done, everyone went their separate ways to handle their business.

It didn't take long for things to run smoothly. Warnock Street was jumping, doing numbers the way Hoc had promised. Jeff opened the block up on Mayfield Street, and already things were picking up. The first two-night shifts did $6,000, and that Friday morning did another $4,000. Within those three days, Mayfield Street did $16,000, and Carlisle Street did it's usual $10,000. Shock just rode through Clearfield Street with twenty young bulls riding dirt bikes and four-wheelers, looking like the modern-day Hells Angels. All of them were wearing motorcycle jackets, with the big biker logo FUCM, "Fuck You, Chase Me," patched on the back. Bay dropped two bricks off on Ruby Street.

Byrd slid down to the Ville to get wit Smitty,

when the news broke through the city that neither Byrd nor Bay knew about. Phones just started ringing, and Byrd's was going off now.

"Byrd, are you anywhere near a TV?" Mary stated calmly.

"Naw, why, what's up?"

"Babe, they just found that girl Shana over there inside the pet cemetery on 11th and Indiana. Babe, the girl was burnt, eaten alive by rats, and her neck was cut open. Inside the hole was two and half ounces of coke with a note that said: 'People live for more, why die for less! PS, WB/WG!'"

"DAMN, I'ma get right back with you, M. Let me make a few calls."

"Alright, be safe. I love you, babe," she replied before ending the call.

RING! RING! RING!

"Yo, bro," Jeff stated into the receiver of his cell phone.

"Honesty, bro, that's your work?"

"Blood in, blood out, American me bro. She won't be the last contestant on that summer jam screen. The bitch turned her nose on some killers, so fuck her, bro. Won't be the first bitch to die behind that nigga."

"Say less, bro! Get with me later on," Byrd said.

"Alright," he replied.

~ ~ ~

RING! RING! RING!

"Rique, WHY? Why you involve my baby? First Monique, and now Shana. Is anyone or anything safe around you? Your own family is dead behind your actions. Now my only daughter is gone." Shana's mother broke down on the other end of the phone. Rique just sat quietly holding his phone pressed against his ear as she vented.

After talking to Shana's mother, Rique floated down Broad Street, deep in thought. Four young bulls were wheeling Banshees past his car. The sounds from the FMF pipes broke his train of thought; then ten dirt bikes came roaring past even louder. A few stood on the seat while wheeling, and one young bull had both legs over the handlebars, with both hands touching the ground, as he slowly walked the bike down Broad Street.

Then Rique noticed Shock zipping through the pack, wheeling toward oncoming traffic down Broad Street. The party of fifteen made a right on Pike Street, heading toward Simon Gratz High School. Rique got jammed up in traffic, not being able to maneuver around the cars the way the bikes were doing.

"Damn," Rique snapped, knowing he missed a good shot.

To his surprise, his shot wasn't missed. It was more like a slipup on his part. Shock had seen Rique's car and maneuvered the pack through traffic. Now seven total bikes were coming up Broad Street, and eight were coming down from behind Rique. Shock was ahead of the pack coming north, and lil Bubby was ahead of the pack coming South. Rique, so caught off guard, but being well seasoned, shot straight into the action, gripping his Glock 27 from underneath his seat.

He maneuvered his car into the direction of the bikes coming south and jumped into the backseat and went ape shit on everything that was coming north, shattering his own back window. Seconds later, Rique was forced back into the front windshield from the impact of his vehicle, sandwiching three four-wheelers up against another car. Without missing a beat, he shot straight into action, jumping out the passenger side door, gun blazing.

BOC! BOC! BOC! BOC! BOC! BOC! BOC! BOC! BOC!

Blood ran down Rique's face. He staggered to gather his feet underneath him and stumbled over the first four-wheeler, which was directly on top of one of Shock's homies.

BOC!

The single slug ripped through shorty's face. Shock and lil Bubby came from around checkers firing their weapons, turning Broad and Butler into a war zone.

BOOM! BOOM! BOOM! BOOM!

BLOCA! BLOCA! BLOCA! BLOCA!

"Can I get a rib platter with mac and cheese . . . ?" Before Ashley could finish placing her order, the big commotion outside brought her attention back to reality. She turned just in time to see all types of four-wheelers and dirt bikes going in every direction.

"What the fuck?" she said to no one in particular.

Two people coming out of the Checkers parking lot on Broad Street off Butler started firing in the direction of a man who was standing directly over someone who was underneath one of the four-wheelers. Not willing to risk her own life, especially on break, Ashley almost turned her attention back to the counter inside Dwight's BBQ joint, until she noticed Shock and saw Rique heading in her direction still firing. Ashley rushed out of the store, pulling out her police issued pistol, and fired.

BOC! BOC! BOC!

Rique noticed the female officer and thought to himself this gotta be one of them bitches, and without a second thought he began throwing shots in her direction.

BOC! BOC! BOC!

Shock saw Ashley and ran straight through Broad Street traffic firing.

BOOM! BOOM! BOOM!

Lil Bubby noticed the cop, but thought to himself if Shock didn't care, fuck it, and lifted his .357 Magnum and fired all six out of his speed loaded magazine.

BOOM! BOOM! BOOM! BOOM! BOOM! BOOM!

This gave Ashley enough time to lock in on Rique, which she did, sending four shots straight through his chest.

BOC! BOC! BOC! BOC!

As Rique's body spun around in a half circle, then collapsed to the ground, Shock was right there upon impact.

BOOM! BOOM! BOOM!

As Ashley approached the scene, Bubby just got finished reloading his speed loader and aimed toward Ashley's face.

"Naw, bro, she folk," Shock stated, stopping him before he parked Ash.

He and Bubby ran back across Broad Street and entered the Checkers parking lot. They jumped back on two brand-new KX-85 dirt bikes and got out of Dodge before the cops arrived.

CHAPTER 9

A FEW DAYS had passed since the news broke about Rique, but it was still business as usual with Boo.

"Naw, bro, that's a bit too high. You gotta understand, if I'm buying a hundred joints at sixteen a piece, I'm not paying more than 17.5 for the other hundred you fronting me. That's respectable, right?"

"Yeah, that's cool!" Det. Gram stated, making sure the audio wiretap was working properly.

"Alright, once I straighten everything out as far as with my folk Rique, I'ma touch base with you no later than next week."

~ ~ ~

"Shock, who the fuck was that boy with you? He damn near shot me. I'm trying to fucking help y'all, and that little light-skinned crazy motherfucker, oh my God," Ash said, shaking her head. "I almost shit my pants once he raised that big-ass gun. I was no more good! I just knew it was over."

Ashley sat inside Bay's living room. Stacy just looked at Ashley like she was crazy, because the little light-skinned crazy person she was speaking of was her lil brother Bubby.

"Ash, you're tripping, that's folks!" Shock stated.

"Well keep his little ass in pocket because I might need him."

"Ashley, you ain't gonna need him, not that one. That's my brother," Stacy stated.

"No, he's not! That little boy is crazy. He better not be your fucking son. You're gonna have major problems with him, girl, real rap."

Just as everybody was fully engaging in conversation, laughing enjoying the company of each other, Bay and Byrd, lil Bubby and Mary walked through Bay's front door tugging two large duffle bags. Jeff and Fatman entered seconds behind them.

"What the fuck is so funny in here, and what's wrong with your face, Ash? It's like you seen a ghost or something. You straight?" Byrd stated, noticing her expression change once they all came through the door.

“Naw, I’m cool. Just seeing that little crazy motherfucker gives me the chills.”

“You ain’t gotta worry, lil buddy, your secret’s safe with me. I ain’t gonna tell nobody you pissed your panties at the sight of this,” little Bubby stated, pulling the .357 Magnum out.

“Boy, put that damn gun away before I beat your ass. You out here riding them damn bikes acting crazy. You gonna give me a goddamn heart attack, and, Bay, you know better, letting him do dumb shit. I promised my mom before she died I wasn’t gonna allow him to turn out like my other brothers. Bubby, you better get your shit together or you’re going down South with Grandma.”

“Alright, Stacy, so answer this, if I ain’t do nothing and Shock got shot, or switch the picture, say it’s Bay, you still want me to sit back and do nothing?”

“No, you better kill somebody,” Stacy stated, frustrated, knowing her baby boy was right and also realizing he was no longer her baby. That's what scared her the most.

"Alright, you finished, Stacy? You got everything out your system, because you gotta understand he's a part of something special now. Ain't no show on earth greater than World Gang. Allow greatness to shine through, we on one."

"Alright, Byrd, you better take special care of this one."

"Got you, baby girl! Don't I make sure Bay return every night?"

"Okay, you made your point, y'all win," Stacy replied.

"Naw, we all win! Now let's break this bread down and eat together," Byrd stated, dumping one of the duffle bags out.

~ ~ ~

"Ab, man this shit crazy old head. Everything me and Boo learned was from watching you and Clark Kent, now I'm trying to kill this nigga. I really wanna sit down and iron this shit out, but my pride old head. What's crazy is, we both know each other's moves, but won't take the shot. I could have iced the nigga out in NY. The nigga called my phone the other day and said he watched me go inside one of my bitch's cribs, then saw my main chick leave and get inside her car."

"Byrd, y'all playing games out here, because for one y'all allowed the streets and money to come between something special. I watched both of you grow into real good lil dudes. Answer this question, would you allow somebody else to kill him?"

"Naw, I'm going ape shit behind that nigga," he replied.

"So, call him, and move past that shit before somebody gets hurt," Ab stated.

"Alright, say less, but for now, let's get down to business. It's time to put the streets on notice. We here now; everything else is old news," Byrd said.

Byrd and Ab was looking around Ab's car lot in search of a few new wheels to prepare for the summer.

"Yo, Bay's really into these Maseratis. Peanut butter guts, this joint's nasty. That's for Ab! I see

Shock fucking with this Range Rover. Get that Camaro for Jeff, because he needs something small for right now, until his wheel game gets up. Oh shit, pull them three 911 Porsches, that's Ash, Mary, and Stacy's right there. Alright I gotta tighten Fatman and lil Bubby up now, so get that Corvette for Fatman and get the . . . naw, fuck it, I'ma give Bubby my Escalade. What's the damage, old head?"

"Naw, don't 'old head' me, we talking money now. You know we talking my language, and I'm not gonna hurt you that much, youngin. I wanna see y'all put on. Listen I wanted fifty-nine for the Maserati, give me forty-five. Give me seventy-three for the Range. I'll take the speed limit (55) for the brand-new Camaro. For the three 911s, give me two ten. Last but not least, the Vette, that's lightweight. Give me forty-five racks."

"God damn, old head, we talking damn near half a ticket, bro, but listen, that ain't really about nothing. Fuck it, can't take this shit with me, right?" Byrd stated, looking at Hoc for confirmation.

"Damn, young buck, you ripping and running

like that out here? I remember you was sitting around wishing for a wishing well."

"Yeah, now I'm throwing bricks inside a fucking wishing well," he joked, happy that he could talk money with Ab.

He remembered those days, just sitting inside his wheel as a kid listening to Ab conduct business, praying for the day his turn would come. Today was that day.

"I got $400k for everything, plus we gone do some other business with you. Special cloth talk, couple whole ones, few properties, and school me as far as that construction company shit goes."

"Show me $400, lil nigga!"

At that very moment, Bubby was coming up Roosevelt Boulevard on a brand-new 2008 Honda TRX 450 four-wheeler, strapping a brand-new Louie Vuitton book bag over his shoulders. He was coming around Rising Sun Avenue, and the only thing that could be heard was the loud FMF pipes headed toward Mateen Auto Sales.

"There it go right there. We do all our trafficking

on ATVs. You know a few young niggas that's gone help you get your bread up are the same young niggas that's gonna help you hit the bread truck," Byrd stated, telling Bubby to toss Ab the bag, then jumping back inside the Audi A8 with Hoc.

~ ~ ~

"June, there's the fucking black kid!"

"Where?" June asked, looking in the wrong direction.

"Right fucking there, white Audi A8, in the passenger seat, turning on the Boulevard."

"Oh yeah, follow that piece of shit," June stated, hitting a few buttons inside his Honda. At that very moment, his dashboard trapdoor opened showcasing two gold Uzis.

"Got it!"

"I got your fucking dummy bag," June stated, snorting line after line of coke.

Right as Hoc entered the Home Depot parking lot, the sound of car tires screeching, horns blowing, and the loud impact of two cars colliding, with Demo zipping through the open space, caught Hoc's and

Byrd's attention.

"Man, Hoc, these niggas gotta be going crazy, all that rushing for some sheetrock and drywall."

"They're weirdos," Hoc said.

"Go ahead and pull inside that open parking spot, before these niggas race for that," Byrd stated.

Right as Hoc made his way toward the spot, Demo raced right in their direction, at an irregular speed.

"Watch out, Hoc. Fuck's wrong with these stupid-ass Ricans?" Just as Byrd made that statement he noticed papi in the Pathmark parking lot. "Oh shit, Hoc, pull out, pull out."

Byrd's statement was cut short from June hanging out the window, mouth and nose covered in white powder. His eyes were the size of fifty cent pieces, as he held onto his Uzi with one hand, then all hell broke loose.

BLACCC! BLACCC! BLACCC! BLACCC! BLACCC!

"I got your fucking paper," he yelled, letting shots off. "Here go some fucking ones too!"

BLACCC! BLACCC!

Byrd and Hoc lay low inside their seats looking through the rearview dash camera. They both watched Demo exit out driver's seat holding the matching Uzi to the one June was spraying, and nervously started firing at the same time while bullets shattered all six windows, ripping through doors, knocking lights out.

"Throw this shit in reverse, Hoc."

On cue, Hoc did as he was told, reversing straight into Demo's body, knocking him straight into the concrete.

"Demo!" June started yelling while still firing out the window.

BLACCC! BLACCC! BLACCC!

"Throw that shit in drive now, Hoc!"

Hoc threw the bullet-holed Audi into drive and maneuvered the car out of the parking lot, back onto Roosevelt Boulevard, then straight across Somerville.

"Damn, bro, you straight? You hit anywhere?" Byrd asked Hoc, checking his own body for holes.

"Naw, I'm cool," Hoc replied, maneuvering throughout the Northeast.

"Freeze, drop the weapon," two Home Depot security guards, squatting behind an old-model Toyota, yelled in the direction of June. He was now standing over Demo's body still snorting more cocaine. "Drop the weapon, stupid motherfucker."

"Freeze, drop the weapon, stupid motherfucker," June repeated sarcastically. "I am froze. I'm ice froze dick head, I mean I'm ice cold. What the fuck can some flashlight cops do to me, bag me for retail theft?" With that statement, June pulled his Uzi back into a firing position and was now on the receiving end of a fresh thirty-two shots, sixteen apiece out of each security guard's standard-issue Ruger pistol.

~ ~ ~

Meanwhile

Bay sat at Broad and Clearfield inside the Exxon gas station, shooting the shit with a thick, red yellow bone, whose ass could double for Nicki Minaj's on any giving Sunday.

"Damn, Trina, so this is what we do, just keep playing games?" Bay stated through Trina's driver's-side window while rubbing his hand against her thigh.

"Bay, stop playing, you know it's gone take a major bag to dance inside this box."

"Man, you got the game fucked up," Bay laughed. "On some real shit, this dick so good I'm the one who shouldn't have to fuck for free."

"See, that's how I know you ain't heavy yet, and I say 'yet' because I'm tuned in."

"Alright, listen, we gone stop playing these cat and mouse games. Get with me now before my stock go through the roof," he stated, reaching up under her skirt and rubbing her pussy.

"Oh shit," she moaned, adjusting her legs a bit, giving him more access to her goodies. "I'm a give you one shot at the title, but don't pick me up inside that," Trina stated, pointing toward Bay's squatter, smiling.

"Oh, you got jokes. This ain't around for long. It's a few coupes coming soon," he stated, moving his finger around a few more times before pulling it out. Her juices followed, wetting the seat of her panties. He lightly kicked the side of Trina's CLS Mercedes Benz.

"Bye, boy, what's your number? I gotta get these kids from daycare."

Bay and Trina exchange numbers, then he jumped inside his Grand Marquis and pulled out of the gas station. Trina made a few quick adjustments to her panties and skirt before pulling out also.

~ ~ ~

"Ross, there's ya man right there," Det. Smart stated.

"Where?" Det. Ross questioned, sitting at the red-light ready to turn right on Clearfield Street.

"Right there, coming out the Exxon gas station, Black Ford Grand Marquis. What do you wanna do, he's headed out our district."

"Fuck what district he's in, today is judgement day. Ain't no district where he's headed."

Det. Ross made the left turn on Broad Street, going across the double lane street, and followed Bay up Park Avenue, onto Allegheny where Bay turned right and headed toward 13th Street.

RING! RING! RING!

"Yo, M," Bay stated into the receiver.

"Bay, check your rearview mirror. I just got a text message from a detective saying his partner took some type of contract from Rique. He's right there behind you," Mary stated, running out of breath trying to get everything out before it was too late.

"What type car they in? It's a few cars behind me right now?"

"Well make some type of turn, Bay. Stop playing games. This ain't the time right now."

Bay could hear the nervousness in Mary's voice and got focused.

"Alright, M, breathe, I got it under control. Call Jeff, naw call lil Bubby and tell him to get to that pet cemetery on 11th Street now and fire on anything that's behind me."

"No, I'm right here on Glenwood and Allegheny. I'ma meet you right there."

"Fuck no, M, call Bubby!"

"Bay, get there, end of conversation," Mary demanded, then ended her call. She rushed through the light. Bay made a right turn on Camac Street, then made another right toward Clearfield. He then turned left underneath the bridge going toward 12th Street. Every turn Bay did, Det. Ross was right there on his heels.

"Ross, do you think he noticed us?" Det. Smart asked.

"Naw, these young fuckers today don't pay that type attention to their surroundings," Ross replied. "Anyway, who gives a flying fuck if he knows I'm behind him, he's mine today."

Bay faked going right on 12th and Glenwood, then hit the left turn signal while going underneath his seat tugging on his Smith and Wesson .40 caliber handgun. He noticed Det. Ross through the rearview mirror and tint.

"Oh, it's this freak! You dumb-ass niggas think I'm slipping out the bitch, huh?" Bay said to himself as he made it to Germantown and Glenwood Avenue. He turned right, heading toward the pet cemetery.

As Bay made it to Germantown and Indiana, he pulled over and parked right there on the corner and called Mary.

"Yeah!"

"Yo, where you at, M?"

"Right here. I'm looking right at you. Ross is getting out behind you now. Just keep walking toward that little block. Start acting like you're looking for the address on one of those houses."

"Alright!"

"Bay," Det. Ross called out, trying to get his attention.

Bay kept walking, faking like he was looking for the right address. He was hoping Mary was ready because the footsteps were getting closer with each step he took. Mary sat squatting down behind an old beat-up car parked in the middle of 10th Street, with her throw-a-way Glock. Byrd gave it to her in case of an emergency. Today was that emergency!

"Bay, you hear me, put your hands above your head now, that's a direct order," Det. Ross yelled out.

Bay kept walking until he noticed Mary squatting

down behind the old Cadillac. He took a few more steps, then spun around, stopping Det. Ross dead in his tracks. He aimed the Smith and Wesson directly at Ross's head.

"What's up? Fuck you keep calling my name for? Do I know you?" Bay asked, giving Mary time to duck walk around the other end of the old car, positioning herself right behind the detective.

She came up slowly, Glock aimed toward the back of Ross's head. She gave Bay a look, letting him know she had the drop on him.

"Huh?"

"What, cat got your tongue? You taking contracts not knowing who you playing with. Go ahead, M, green light."

Det. Ross couldn't believe his fate and thought he had heard Bay wrong. He never heard anybody else come up behind him. Out of nervousness and fear Ross didn't want to turn around, but thought better of it and did so, just in time to catch Mary's face. He saw the blue flame and heard what sounded like thunder ringing off inside his ear.

BOC! BOC! BOC! BOC!

Bay stood over what remained of Det. Ross's head, then tried to stop Mary from shaking. He removed the Glock from her trembling hands and looked Mary directly in her eyes.

"Thank you," he mumbled to her, before focusing his attention back to Det. Ross. He fired the remaining six rounds into his body.

BOC! BOC! BOC! BOC! BOC! BOC!

CHAPTER 10

"DAMN, KEISHA, THIS shit crazy," Keen stated, with his eyes rolling in the back of his head.

Keisha knew in order to get something done, you had to use your brain. That's exactly what she was doing now, positioned between Keen's legs inside his Nissan Maxima. She was licking underneath the shaft of his dick, her tongue circling his balls, then back up, making sure she coated her mouth with enough spit. Her actions left saliva running back down onto his balls before she reached the head, vacuum cleaning everything back up on her way down.

"God damn, Keisha," Keen stated as she went down, head hitting the horn. He sat at the light, for three red lights, not able to move, with cars beeping their horns trying to get them to proceed. There was no way Keen could move. His foot and leg was locked on the brake pedal as Keisha maneuvered her mouth and allowed her tongue to work its magic. She squeezed the base of his dick and sucked every ounce of cum out of his pickle.

"Mmmmm," she moaned.

"God damn, Keisha, you're good."

"I know," she stated.

"What's up though? You never gave me the time of day before, now this?" Keen asked her.

"Naw, our timing wasn't right. I was chasing behind a few ghosts, but I need you now. Ain't nobody else gone do shit behind my brother being killed, and I know Byrd did that shit. You was Green's youngin, and I know you ain't scared, right?"

"Fuck no, ain't one scared bone inside this body," Keen stated.

Deep down he didn't really want to test the waters as far as going to war, but Keisha was right, Green was his old head. It was time to change the speed and put work in.

~ ~ ~

Upstate, in Buffalo New York, the weather wasn't that bad as Boo stepped out of his car and headed toward Fresh Start for Legs Rehabilitation Center.

Upon entering the front door, Boo noticed people all around, some with and some without legs and arms, but the energy inside that facility was magical. There was nothing but hard-working staff, and clients working toward becoming rehabilitated. Rique sat in the corner in his wheelchair doing nothing but staring out the window.

"Damn, bro, I drove all these miles thinking I was gone assist you as far as getting back mobile, and you're sitting by this fucking window star gazing. Success ain't out there; it's inside that lap pool."

"Listen, bro, if you drove all this way just to come grind me up, well today ain't that day," Rique stated, while still looking out the window into no man's land.

"You're right, I'm done trying if you're cool being a fucking sit-down clown. That's your life, but just fucking know them same niggas who put you inside that chair are waiting on your return. They out there waiting to put you six feet deep then ground level. If you're cool with that, so am I. Don't ask me to be your wheelchair partner or grave neighbor, because my future say hammer shit: kill or be killed. Ain't nothing inside my cards say shit about being inside no rehab or looking out no window searching for no pity party."

"Nigga, fuck you. If my legs was working you wouldn't dare say no shit like that, pussy," Rique stated, frustrated, shaking his chair trying to stand up, but not being able to as light tears rolled down his cheek.

"Man, save that energy and remove yourself from this place."

Boo headed straight toward the parking lot, leaving Rique there to gather his thoughts and figure his own problems out.

RING! RING!

"Yo, who this?"

"Damn, just that quick you erase good nigga's voice straight out your head. I've been sitting with a few good niggas saying this was a much-needed call, so without further ado, here I am."

"Damn, last, I checked, you ain't have no conscious. You allowed a nigga we grew up with to throw sixty shots at me?"

"Come on!"

"Naw, listen! What you think, I'm supposed to sit back, say, 'Damn, this Byrd calling,' and everything that was done, fuck it?"

"We both still breathing. Ain't nothing wrong with what they did. Nigga, you fucking crazy."

"See, it's your pride, because first and foremost you wasn't never supposed to get involved. You allowed paper to separate a bond we created years ago, nigga."

"What fucking bond, bro?"

"Remember, nigga, me and you dropped shit together. That's a fucking bond. Sleeping head to foot, that's a fucking bond, nigga. When you tried to take me off this fucking earth, all I see is another face between three dots over this forty, nigga. You and Bay are fucking targets now. You know the fucking rules, mount up!"

"Damn, bro, I came in peace, but that's your

word, say less. You're right, I do know the rules. Give Rique my best wishes. Oh, and don't think it can't happen out in Buffalo, nigga."

Click! The line went dead.

With that being said, Byrd left Boo standing there wondering how the hell he knew he was out in Buffalo. That very thought made Boo clutch a little tighter around his pistol underneath his black Versace hoodie.

~ ~ ~

"Bay, this nigga ain't trying to hear that shit," Byrd stated, sitting in the passenger seat of Bay's Maserati, blowing sour diesel out the window on Warnock Street.

"Man, fuck that nigga, bro. Fuck what Ab talking about too, and fuck what Clark Kent talking about. Them niggas ain't the ones mounting up. If that's the nigga's word, we'll cross that bridge once we see him, and it's light out."

"You right, say less," Byrd replied, making a call to Shock on his cell phone.

"Yo, bro!"

"Ah, man, cousin, they can't say I didn't try. The nigga's pride's too big. Go ahead, you have the green light."

"Consider it done," Shock said into the receiving end of the phone. He was sitting outside of Boo's daughter's daycare, where her and Rique's son attended.

At that very moment, Shock and lil Bubby were watching both kids run throughout the open play area, carefree, around a bunch of other little three- and four-year-old kids.

"Damn, Shock, this nigga Byrd this cold? I really ain't built for this type of shit. Harming little babies ain't really my speed, but I ain't gone leave you naked out this bitch," Bubby said, not really feeling this mission.

As thoughts ran through his head of his own little cousins and soon-to-be nephew, Shock walked straight into the play area, right up to Boo's daughter.

"Hey, ain't you Angel? I'm good friends with your dad. He told me to come pick you up today, and it's a surprise. You ain't gonna tell him I told you about the surprise, are you?" Shock smiled, speaking baby talk.

"No, I promise, I won't tell him!" lil Angel stated, jumping up and down waiting for Shock to break the good news.

"Well, okay, today they're throwing you and your cousin baby Rique a party at Chuck E. Cheese's. A lot of little princesses gone be there and everything. You ready to go?"

"Yes, yes, yes!" little Angel replied excitedly, jumping up and down.

"Alright, go get baby Rique, and we're leaving."

Angel ran off so fast, and returned even faster. Her and baby Rique were back in record-breaking time. They headed out of the play area hand in hand with Shock, smiling from ear to ear singing we're going to Chuck E. Cheese's. Lil Bubby open the back door while Shock carefully strapped both kids inside their seat belts then shut the door. He jumped back in the passenger seat and dialed Byrd's number.

"Yo, what's up, baby boy?"

"The coast is clear, bro. I'm with the little brats

right now. They jumping up and down inside their seats thinking about Chuck E Cheese's. Ain't y'all thinking about Chuck E. Cheese's!" Shock asked Boo's daughter and Rique son.

"Yes!" both kids screamed in unison, getting more excited.

"Alright, hold on a minute. Let me three-way this nigga real quick."

Byrd wanted to see if the tone in that nigga Boo's voice would change up once he heard lil Angel's voice.

"Yo, bro, you really don't get the picture! Ain't no more rapping. Fuck you keep calling back on some freak shit for? You said you know my location, then stop punching while I'm in traffic and send that shit in my direction so I can send one of you niggas back crip walking."

"Damn, bro, you finished talking? Because I hate talking over people. This phone call ain't about you. I heard you loud and clear. You wanna take it to that next level, right? Well listen to this. Who wanna go to Chuck E. Cheese's?" Byrd said away from his phone.

"We do, we do!"

"Angel, tell your dad you know about the surprise party. He ain't mad."

"Dad, you ain't are you?" lil Angel asked into the phone, still jumping up and down inside the backseat.

"Byrd, come on, bro, we ain't never play no family games," Boo stated, pulling over to the shoulder of the road. "That's my baby girl, cousin."

"Oh, I know. Remember, I know who you really love, nigga. Ain't no more games. Fuck keeping on chasing behind you niggas. I'ma teach my young niggas how you bring monsters back down to earth. The sport changed, nigga. Ain't nothing safe out this bitch. Remember I told you to give Rique my best wishes? Well fuck that! I got his son too, so spend back around and break the news to his crippled ass too. Go ahead, young, put that blindfold on both of them and put the headphones in both of their ears, then walk them off the platform at the nearest train station," Byrd stated.

"Byrd, you do that, bro, I swear ain't no turning

back. I'ma kill everything you love, bro," Boo stated, tears rolling down his face. He thought about the day Angel came into this world, and what kind of joy her little soul had brought to his life. The thought that Byrd might bring this type of pain to his life only fueled his fire more.

"Damn, bro, you're quiet as shit now. What, cat got your fucking tongue now?"

"I'm here," he mumbled with a lump in his throat.

"Listen, I'm a do you a major favor, bro. Don't say I ain't never do shit for you in your most devastating moments. Listen, step out the wheel and walk into the oncoming traffic, and I'll let her and Rique's son go right now."

Shock broke into the conversation again, "Yo, Byrd, we right here at Broad and Erie under the subway station now. The express train looks like it's coming from Allegheny now. What's next?"

"Boo, you heard him, nigga, what's next? You gonna play in traffic, or allow them kids to play chicken with this fucking train?" Byrd asked. "You know what, fuck that nigga, youngin'. Go ahead and send them on their way. We'll catch that nigga in traffic."

"Byrd!!!!"

It was already too late. Boo's cries fell on deaf ears. Even if Byrd wanted to stop the shit, the express train was entering the tunnel blowing its horn and Angel's and lil Rique's feet just touched the yellow line of the platform. Shock stuck his phone in the air allowing Boo and Byrd to hear all the commotion going on under the subway station. A bunch of screaming people shouting, "Oh no!" and "Somebody call the police," then the emergency button sound and screeching noises let Boo and Byrd know shit was serious.

"Oh, my fucking God, his head looked like it went straight to Hunting Park."

"Please, please somebody call the police! HELP! SOMEBODY PLEASE CALL 911, PLEASE!" the elder lady kept screaming. She couldn't believe what she just witnessed right there in front of her.

"Boo, you still there, nigga? I know you still

there. Listen, bro, I know you're speechless. It's gonna be alright, nigga. Just breathe, bro. Inhale, exhale, envision her little soul floating, but also envision her little light ass getting hit from Erie Avenue to Olney, nigga. Now mount up, pussy, we'll be waiting." Byrd laughed then ended the phone call.

"Damn, bro, ain't no turning back now. It's on!" Bay said, pulling out of the parking lot.

CHAPTER

11

"MAN, FUCK THAT nigga! I gave them too many chances. I can't keep playing with these niggas out here, bro. Every time I turn around they're doing some lame shit. You got these nut-ass papis throwing shit in my direction because I'm out here slipping, worried about these niggas. Clark Kent supposed to line this meeting up with this nigga Champ from down South Philly. Supposedly he heavy as far as them joints. I'ma fuck with Ab and see if it's something successful that could come from that end. I'm supposed to meet him over his tag and insurance joint on Hunting Park. Young, it's too much shit on the table to keep playing with Boo and Rique," Byrd stated.

"Listen, my man Louie gotta super gun line that's heavy. This shit you just started we gotta really mount up now and finish it," Bay stated, knowing shit was serious now. "Byrd, you know ain't no secrets between gang, bro. I really didn't get the chance to scream at you, but remember that Detective Ross character? Br, that was me and M who dropped that nigga. Ashley just got the address as far as the niggas partner. We gotta drop him too, bro."

"Damn, young, I really don't care what's going on. Don't hold that type of information hostage, bro, because she's out here working like she ain't just do that shit."

"Byrd, she ain't been working, she scared shitless," Bay said, turning left on 12th and Poplar Street heading toward the church for something to eat.

"My baby shitting bricks, huh?" Byrd stated. Him and Bay broke out into a light laugh knowing how scared of a person Mary was, then both entered the basement of the church. The beautiful smell of baked mac and cheese, fried chicken, and candied yams hit their noses all at once.

"Damn, Byrd, this shit worth the risk, bro! You know I've been going through it with the nigga Sherm from Richard Allen Projects."

"Bay, you really got a lot of shit going on I really don't know about."

~ ~ ~

A few months later

Things had been heating up after the news about Boo's and Rique's kids broke out, plus Det. Smart and Det. Ross being successfully killed. Now Byrd, Shock, Bay, and Jeff were wanted for questioning on multiple murders. Det. Smart was found under the bridge on 17th and Indiana inside an unmarked police car burnt to a crisp. His own police-issue .45 pistol was stuck inside his mouth. There was a hole the size of a tennis ball in the back of his head. Rique's main young bull, lil Sean, was found in a Bojack Boys Construction lot on 15th Street, neck deep in the dirt. Once CSI started to dig up his body, to their surprise there wasn't a body, only lil Sean's head remained there.

Two nights later, his body without the head was hanging from the basketball court at the playground. A couple weeks later, lil Bubby's body was found in front of the 39th District in the trunk of a Camaro, with two bullet holes to his head. The streets were in a major uproar because the same night Stacy was to identify Bubby's body, she was gunned down across the street from Temple University Hospital.

"Calling all cars! Dispatch, we're in pursuit of one of the defendants. He's operating a motor vehicle on the 3100 block of North 16th Street. Recognizing and having no doubt in mind that the operator is the same male wanted on a body warrant for the homicide warrant that was issued on 3-13-08. We attempted to stop the vehicle by activating our lights and sirens, but the operator failed to comply. I need full backup, I repeat full backup! The vehicle is beginning to move at a very high rate of speed, swerving in and out of traffic, traveling into the oncoming lanes. Now he's disregarding numerous stop signs and red lights. Where's the fucking backup?"

The pursuit continued through approximately four city police districts, leading to Shock leaving the motorcycle on Hope Street. He fled on foot through the alleyway and successfully got away.

~ ~ ~

"Detective Gregory, I've just faxed SCI Huntingdon a subpoena, requesting a recording of any and all incoming and outgoing telephone calls to or from inmate James Williams FT-5573. The recording time requested is from the date of intake, which is 12-21-07 to present. Refer to homicide case M07-294."

"Damn, Paul, we had that fucking kid yesterday. There's no way that little bastard should have gotten away on that fucking motorbike. He was cornered in, but caught another major break, because the kid T-Roy used the phone twenty to thirty times daily. This morning we heard him saying he's supposed to get released Thursday, and Byrd's wife or girl, if I ain't mistaken, is supposed to be his ride home. If we get a warrant to tail whoever's car it is, I'll bet that it leads us straight to Byrd," Det. Brown stated.

~ ~ ~

Inside the Philadelphia medical examiner's office, the body of Ashley was being examined by two MEs.

“Dr. Bradley, what do we have here today?” Dr. Hines asked.

“A single gunshot wound to the right lateral posterior chest wall, one half by three eighths inch, without soot or stippling, no upper body garment. Through the right middle lung lobe hilum of the right lung, right upper lung lobe, T3 and T1 vertebral bodies without spinal cord injury into the left side of the neck (thoracic inlet) with injury perforation of the left upper lung lobe and subclavian vessels with minimal hemoaspiration into the left lung as well as pallor of the visceral organs. This poor girl never saw it coming,” Dr. Bradley stated, placing a tag on Ashley’s toe.

“Well at least she didn’t have to suffer,” Dr. Hines replied as he watched Dr. Bradley finishing up the autopsy.

“I’m going to turn my final reports over to the district attorney’s office once it’s complete. They want to have everything prepared once the assailants are caught. They think they have an open-and-shut case," Dr. Bradley said.

"Well let's not disappoint them then," Dr. Hines joked.

Everything had to be in order when it came to presenting the findings of an autopsy. All the I's had to be dotted, and the T's had to be crossed. Any kind of mistakes, and the killer or killers would end up getting off. The doctors were very precise with every detail of the body, recording everything. Once they finished, they covered the corpse up, then went to lunch.

CHAPTER 12

SUCCESSFULLY DODGING A few traps and major police manhunts, Byrd and T-Roy sat parked on a small little block right off 52nd and Parkside, inside Byrd's triple black Jaguar with 5 percent tinted windows.

"Damn, bro, honestly, I'm glad you touched down, but the timing couldn't be worse. Everything around us feels like the walls are closing in, bro. I haven't even spoken with Bay in days, and then Boo, Rock, Stacy, and Ashley, so ain't really no way as far as comfort, dig me?"

"So, what happened with the young bull Bubby?" T-Roy asked, looking out the Jaguar window, and focusing his attention on a dark car that circled around the block a few times.

"Bro, honestly, shorty ain't leave me no choice. I told Shock to walk the niggas' kids off the platform. This nigga Bubby got cold feet, tried to grab the kids and knocked some old-ass man off the platform in front of thc fucking train," Byrd stated.

"So, what's up with the kids?"

"Mary took them down to Atlanta, to her mom's crib. I told her don't come back up unless I get killed or booked, and if I was killed, rock them."

"Damn, so listen, Byrd, fuck me just coming home. Let's move like the old days. Tell Shock, Bay, and Jeff to turn themselves in. Once they get their discovery, it will contain all the necessary information, like witness addresses, and their names, but you gotta get a lawyer that's willing to play ball, 'cause he gotta get family members' information too, bro."

"Alright, I gotta get these lil niggas to buy all the way in and trust the process. We gone clean everything up, and still handle everything else."

Byrd finished making his statement, and T-Roy jumped on the wheel and then headed toward Parkside. He made the right-hand turn on 52nd Street, heading in the direction of Osage Avenue.

~~~

A few miles away, in North Philly
~~~

Fully back to his regular physical strength, Rique sat inside the living room of his aunt Cheddar's house on 13th and Somerset, loading up an AK-47 assault rifle and two Glock 40 handguns with extended thirty-shot magazines.

"Aunt Cheddar, listen, don't let little Mal and them play around in the basement. I got some different shit down there, alright?"

"Boy, ain't nobody going down there. Just don't be running back and forth through the house at all different times of the night, because ain't nobody got time for the dumb shit, Rique. You're my sister's only boy, so I won't turn my back on you. But, Rique, don't bring that goddamn drama here, you hear me boy?" Cheddar stated, knowing he was getting ready to do some stupid shit.

"Cheddar, you tripping," Rique stated, heading out the door, carrying a Hugo Boss duffle bag containing the AK-47 assault rifle. He jumped straight into his Mercedes Benz G-Wagon.

~ ~ ~

"Yeah, this Champ, right? Yeah, this Clark Kent,

young bull. I got caught up in traffic. You already know my situation, so I can't really be floating around like that. Listen, where you wanna meet at, North Philly or down South Philly? Alright, well listen, my sister stay on Tucker Street, right there off Lehigh Avenue. There's a little car wash right there on Broad Street, you can't miss it. Just come down 15th Street. Alright, say less, bro. I'ma have the paper already bagged up," Byrd stated into the receiving end of his phone.

~ ~ ~

30 minutes later

Byrd sat on the corner of 15th and Lehigh, on his black Suzuki Hayabusa motorcycle, waiting for Champ to pull up. The duffle bag was stationed underneath a nearby car, containing $450k. At that moment, the black Ford F-150 pickup truck was crossing Lehigh. Byrd lifted the visor up on his helmet giving Champ the sign it was him. Champ followed the motorcycle around Tucker Street.

"Damn, y'all got North on fire, if it wasn't for

Clark Kent. Trust me, bro, I wouldn't even cross city hall for you."

"Who you telling, bro? I wouldn't cross city hall for my damn self-right now, but the show don't stop, I gotta feed niggas in these streets," Byrd replied.

As Niesha came out of her crib and looked under the nearby car, she grabbed the bag and walked to Champ's truck. She waited for the other bag and walked back off in the direction of her house.

"Listen, from now on you gone get with my sister. I can't keep playing in traffic like this. You ain't gotta worry, the paper ain't gone never be twisted or short. Everything gone be super straight," Byrd stated, turning the motorcycle engine back on. He shook Champ's hand, beeped the horn at Niesha, and proceeded up the block slowly, respecting the law, and threw it in second letting the engine scream—fuck the cops. He turned right on 16th Street and shot straight across Lehigh Avenue.

~ ~ ~

"Man, T-Roy, you and Byrd fucking tripping. Man, fuck that, ain't no fucking way I'm locking myself up for no fucking ten homicides. They throwing niggas under the jail for one. Fuck you think they gone do about a fucking dime, nigga? It's Pinesaw, locked in twenty-three, out one, like Pelican Bay, nigga," Bay stated, looking around at Shock and Jeff to agree with him and quoting Denzel Washington from the movie *Training Day*.

"Man, listen, you got my word, bro, on everything. Won't none of y'all do over two years. I'ma mop everything up. Y'all's job is getting money, my job is killing shit. Now if we all out here going ape shit, when the dust settles and the smoke clears, we all gone be behind the wall saying we should of did it this way," Troy stated.

"Fuck it, Bay, you wanna stay out this bitch, go 'head. Ain't nobody forcing nothing down your throat. I know you wanna be the one to return Boo that favor for Stacy, but it ain't about that. We gang if you get him or I get him. You think I want y'all niggas behind them fucking walls? Nigga, I need y'all out here. It's us against the world. We're gonna mop everything up once y'all get those discoveries."

"Alright, I swear, Byrd, this shit better work. That nigga iced my family bro, Stacy and Bubby," he stated as the party of five sat around, all on Hondas and Hayabusa motorcycles right off Kelly Drive.

~ ~ ~

March 21, 2008

"The beginning of a purge, reporting live from 22nd and Hunting Park. We're here live outside the 39th District Police Headquarters, where dozens of media outlets and reporters are taking photos of three murdering terrorist organization members of a well-known North Philly gang, known as World Boys, who are being escorted by their attorneys and police into the district, to be processed and charged for twenty-six homicides."

"Bay, right here, I'm reporting for *The Philadelphia Times*. Did you murder your own child's mother? Did you kill Detective Ross? Did you kill your child's mother's little brother?"

"Over here, Shock, I'm reporting for CNN. Did you assist lil Steve a.k.a. Bubby in the murder of

James Rudy, a sixty-eight-year-old man who was pushed over the platform at Broad and Erie Avenue subway station?"

"No questions will be answered at this time. My client is an innocent civilian," Shock's attorney said while the party of three was escorted into the district all wearing black World Boy hoodies and black ski masks.

Across the Street was Byrd and T-Roy, dressed in matching black hoodies, black jeans, and suede black Timberland boots. A motorcycle helmet was on Byrd's head so he could go unnoticed. T-Roy's helmet was stationed on his Yamaha R1 gas tank.

"Damn, bro, this shit super serious, cousin. We gotta get straight to work. You see this shit? They got an anti-World Boy protest going on. Them niggas must of been really setting shit on fire out here," T-Roy stated, starting his motorcycle engine up.

"Believe me, bro, they ain't seen shit yet 'bout them three little niggas that walked through that door. I'ma purge out this bitch, bro, real wrap."

With that statement Byrd brought his Hayabusa

to life and took off down Hunting Park toward Broad Street, with T-Roy following right behind him. Both of them weaved in and out of different lanes, disregarding the speed limited for operating a motor vehicle on public inner-city streets. Purge was the new retaliation in their minds.

"Yo, M, what's up, baby?" Byrd said into his phone. "Yeah, they walked through them doors like soldiers. Couldn't be me, stink, real rap, but they got more faith in me than anything, so I ain't got no choice."

"Why they wear them damn hoodies and masks? Y'all always up to no good. I bet that was Bay's idea. I'm sitting here watching CNN now. My grandma was like, 'Who the hell is that?' She gone say, 'What's wrong with today's world? Young people turning theyself in, in guilty clothes now," Mary said, missing Byrd, wondering inside her head if she should just leave the kids down South and go back to Philly with him.

"Why you ain't tell your grandma that was your family on TV and they're innocent civilians who right now are miss judged? Listen, stink, we've been on this phone long enough, plus I'm sitting here at McDonald's on some sitting duck shit . . . Naw, the one on Broad and Diamond . . . Alright, I love you too!" As soon as he ended the call, his cell went off again.

"Byrd, Boo is right here on 12th Street talking to my cousin. I'ma stall him out until you get here. How long you gone be?" Niesha asked.

"Five minutes! Listen, Nye, once you see my bike coming down the street, I need you to get low immediately, real rap. Grip your folks as soon as you see the bike."

"Alright, alright!"

With that being said, Byrd started the motorcycle's engine. He whipped the MAC-90 machine gun around toward the front of his chest, underneath his Polo vest. He double-checked Broad Street's traffic, then shot straight out of McDonald's parking lot.

"Damn, Boo, you really gone act like you don't see me right here? That's crazy," Niesha said.

"Naw, it ain't like that, Nye! I wouldn't never front on you. Just me and your folks was screaming about some important shit. Plus, after I was finished talking I had plans for you coming with me anyway," Boo replied.

"Bye, boy, you ain't ready," Niesha smirked, giving Boo a look that it was on. If he only knew the true meaning of her look, he wouldn't be thinking about no pussy, but a way to get the fuck out of there.

Cutting through traffic, Byrd made the right-hand turn on Cumberland, shot down toward 13th Street, made the left, and shot straight toward Lehigh, then made another right-hand turn. Niesha could hear the pipes way before Byrd even turned down 12th Street. Just the aggressiveness from the growl coming from the Hayabusa allowed her to know shit was getting ready to turn ugly, and she did as Byrd told her.

"Alex, come here real quick. Boo ain't going nowhere. I fucking dropped my earring under this stupid-ass car, trying to roll this weed up for you. I knew I should have took my ass inside the house."

"Nye, don't blame that shit on me. Hold up,

Boo," Niesha's cousin stated, bending down under the car with Niesha. At just that moment Byrd turned on 12th Street and saw Boo's Mercedes CL-63 BRABUS Kit Benz parked directly in front of Niesha cousin's door. He unzipped his Polo vest, exposing the MAC-90 that was strapped around his shoulders, and slid down 12th Street in second gear. He coasted with his left hand holding the clutch and right hand wrapped around the mini machine gun. Just as he approached the Benz from behind, Boo was stepping out the driver's side door.

"Fuck, y'all need some . . ." Before Boo could finish his statement, all hell broke loose.

BLACCC! BLACCC! BLACCC! BLACCC! BLACCC!

A few people started scattering in different directions. An old drunk holding a can of 211 Steel Reserve beer was the first to get shot directly in his face. He also caught other bullets that ripped through his entire body,

BLACCC! BLACCC! BLACCC!

One of the bullets exited out of the back of his

head, causing his body to collapse sideways onto a light pole. The next few shots gave Byrd enough time to jump off his bike and shatter every window out of Boo's Benz, as he followed a now crawling Boo around the trunk. Boo was throwing shot's behind him wildly.

BOC! BOC! BOC!

Byrd aimed toward Boo's car tire and fired. The single shot knocked any and all air out of the tire, causing the driver's side rear to come down smashing Boo's hand under the tire, giving Byrd enough time to approach.

"Byrd, no, no, please, it ain't worth it. It's too many people out here. I swear they gone tell on you," Niesha's cousin yelled.

Byrd stood over top of Boo's body, aiming his MAC-90 toward his head. His childhood flashed before his eyes: them running through abandoned houses, partying girls together, and running from cops together. As Byrd look down, Boo was reaching under the car in search of his pistol that he dropped. Byrd's thoughts were now removed from his mental.

He was more clear-headed than ever now. He looked Boo directly in the eyes, hearing police sirens approaching, and fired.

BLOC! BLOC! BLOC!

Just as the first shot was going off, Niesha's cousin knocked Byrd's arm sideways sending the MAC-90 firing toward a sea of police cars coming down 12th Street.

"Byrd, go now," Niesha started yelling. Breaking out of his trance, Byrd backpedaled, firing while jumping back on the Hayabusa motorcycle. He took off down 12th Street at a very high rate of speed, banging down Cumberland Street the wrong way, then turned on Park Avenue and made another right headed toward Broad Street.

~ ~ ~

"Figga, Reed, and Davis, leave your stuff sitting there. You have an official visit," the CO replied as soon as they entered the quarantine block. They had just come up from being processed in CFCF.

"What? That's what I'm talking about."

"Damn, y'all haven't even been fully processed

through and already official visits. Some of these niggas can't even pay $330 bails. Don't worry, I'm a put y'all on the same block, A-1-3. My girlfriend, Boss, is over there. I'ma call and let her know y'all coming," a super-thick light-skinned CO stated. "I seen y'all's shit this morning on the news. I hope you beat that shit."

"Damn, what's your name? I'ma let your girlfriend know we only fucking with you. You already know what we need," Bay stated.

"Alright, I got you. Go 'head because it's too many eyes on y'all right now."

With that being said, Bay, Jeff, and Shock followed another CO through a few doors and inside the visiting room. Once inside, three attorneys were standing there waiting for them.

"Good evening, gentleman. I've been retained by a great friend of mine to represent you. Excuse me, gentleman, but, officer, this is attorney-client confidentiality. There are a few things we're going to go over that are only for me and my clients to know, so with all due respect, I would appreciate it if you'd allow us a few minutes for a private conversation."

The correctional officer exited the visiting room, leaving the three attorneys and their clients alone.

"Now, as I was saying, your discoveries won't be ready until mid-way through the trial, but I've pulled a few strings in the district attorney's office and pulled the list of names that are on your cases. Bay, you have ten witnesses: James Scott a.k.a. Pooh, Henry Ray a.k.a. Sharp, and Felisha White a.k.a. Star, are your star witnesses. Everybody else made minor statements just saying they heard shots but didn't see the shooter. One witness is in protective custody; he's a well-known rat. He does nothing but jump on other people's cases."

"So, who is this motherfucker, so we can handle this shit before it's too late? I'll be damned if I'm going to prison for some jailhouse snitch."

"He's a killer for the DA. His name is Kenneth Ruff a.k.a. Kenny. He's on all three of y'all cases from behind these walls, saying a young guy from the neighborhood who was in lockup with him told him about every murder y'all did. That's why it's so necessary to handle him quick."

"Shock, you're actually cool," his attorney said. "It was actually the guy Bubby pushing the old man off the platform. The DA just wants to make some type of agreement with you for a deal, if you return the kids on tape that Bubby grabbed off the platform."

"Jeff, honestly, there's no evidence against you. A few people had been down to homicide saying you did a few murders. Somehow everybody who entered homicide never was found for a follow-up statement, so you're actually good. It's just a waiting process! They have y'all on twenty-six murders, but only have evidence on ten. Now you have the same information as them. Next week I'll have the names of every officer involved in all the cases."

"Man, fuck that. How on God's green earth could they book us for twenty-six murders but only have enough evidence for ten? That means the only ten murders they have is on me," Bay stated.

"Yeah, right, but now they're looking at the organization as a national security threat. It's basically every last one of you against the Philadelphia Police Department. Before, y'all were winning, so now the PPD and FBI are joining as allies in order to make sure y'all don't become too successful. They don't understand how y'all stayed under the radar so long, yet managed to commit as many murders without slipping up and getting caught. Now the higher ups are breathing down their necks for results. Here is stage one of those results, fellas," Jeff's attorney said, speaking frankly.

"This shit's serious, bro. They just lock us in like some undocumented immigrants, waiting to be deported back to the slave ship. Listen, I appreciate the time and energy. Tell our good friend we straight," Bay began saying to their attorneys. "Let him know we got the ten grand on our books, plus we got $3,000 apiece lining the elastic of our drawers. Tell him in about twenty-four hours we should all be online."

They shook all three attorneys' hands and headed toward the metal door. Bay kicked it with his Prada sneaker, giving the signal to the officer on the other side that they were ready to leave the visiting room and be escorted back to their new cell block.

"Wait, wait, take this legal folder with you. There are a few key things inside that all three of you might necessarily need. You're all going to the same block, right?" Shock's attorney asked, handing the large yellow envelope over. It read "Client/Attorney Use Only" in big bold letters.

"Yeah, we're going on A-1-3, wherever the fuck that is," Jeff replied.

The correctional officer opened the door and waited as all three men came strolling out of the visiting room smiling. They were wearing orange jumpsuits and black Prada sneakers.

"Damn, bro, that's crazy how they handled y'all's situation in the media, if what your attorneys were saying is the truth," said the CO that was walking them down the corridor, headed toward A-1-3.

Bay and Jeff just looked at each other smirking, knowing exactly what the CO was trying to do, and they weren't biting the bait. There wouldn't be any conversation about their case to open the doors for him making some money.

“Listen, bro, we had a crazy day. Maybe under different circumstances, and I mean maybe, I might entertain the convo. Right now, we just trying to fall dead inside a cell for right now and gather our thoughts on some different shit. That jailhouse shit gotta wait a few days, real talk,” Shock stated.

“Yeah, that’s understandable! Just tell Boss I said get with me if y’all need anything.”

At that very moment the sally port doors slid open, and the three of them walked onto the block to get their cell assignments from the officer on duty. It was CO Boss!

“Reed, Figga, Davis—listen, Ciera called up here and said put y’all three inside the same cell. I had to make a few adjustments, so y’all going inside cell 9. Now which one of you was fucking her, because she turned her nose down at every nigga that shot some shit in her direction.”

“Didn’t none of us fuck shorty, but if we did, pillow talking ain’t something we do. She just respect real ones. That's it, Ms. Boss," Bay replied, smirking as he headed toward cell 9, with Jeff and Shock right on his heels. Shock was holding onto the yellow envelope their lawyer gave them.

"Damn, bro, these fucking cells little as shit. Where the fuck am I supposed to sleep, and what the fuck is this?" he asked, pointing toward the boat bed that was lying on the floor.

"Man, go ahead, you got the bunk. You don't know nothing about that boat life, bro! You gotta turn that joint into something." Jeff laughed, reaching for the three commissary boxes and sliding the boat on top of them.

"Shock, fuck is this nigga talking about? This nigga offending me. Byrd better be right about this shit, 'cause if I gotta live like this, it's on, bro," Bay stated.

CHAPTER 13

Two days later

BYRD AND T-ROY sat at the top of Hicks Street right off the dead end of Indiana Avenue, inside Byrd's triple black Jaguar.

"Damn, bro, you serious? Ain't no way the little young bull Keen fell for that type of banana in the tailpipe shit. Shorty ain't even a respectable bitch. How did he let lil Keisha put him under the gun like that, especially at this time. Everybody in the city knows I ain't playing right now," Byrd stated.

"Cousin, these young bulls be doing shit we would never understand, but believe this, it's a lesson that's going to be learned. The nigga should of let the lil bitch suck him off and kept it pushing. He should have never accepted those terms and conditions. Then my lil young girl was saying Keisha's going around saying Keen forced Bay, Jeff, and Shock to take lock-up. Like these niggas was already booked and went to the bucket."

"Listen, bro, this is how it's going down: You clean lil Keisha up. I got the young bull Keen, bro. I'ma teach him how this big-boy league works. It's really levels to this shit," Byrd stated, pulling the Jag out of the dirt lot to drop T-Roy off at his grandma's house in the middle of Indiana.

Once T-Roy shut the door, Byrd noticed another nigga on his hit list coming out of another house a few doors down from T-Roy's grandma house. They locked eyes for a few seconds while Byrd cruised the Jag toward Broad Street checking his rearview mirror.

~ ~ ~

"Rip the lining like this, bro," Jeff stated, showing Shock and Bay how to get the money out quickly without completely destroying their underwear. "I'm telling y'all now, if we don't get no visit soon, they're gonna be your only drawers for a few days."

"Nigga, you tripping. Shock, hit that call button. Tell the CO chick something wrong with the sink and can she come down real quick. Watch this boss shit, bro!" Bay said, completely ripping his drawers to get his money.

Shock hit the call button and then went over to the desk and told CO Boss what Bay said, and the two of them headed back toward their cell.

"What's wrong with y'all's sink, boy, because everything was working fine when the other people left. Don't tell me you done came right in breaking shit," CO Boss stated, standing at the door with one hand on her hip, chewing gum.

"Yeah, this joint crazy! I put this hundred-dollar bill inside the drain hole trying to stop this shit up so I could take a light bird bath before laying in my bed, because you can't sleep smelling like these niggas, but that's really neither here nor there. Listen, I just realized we ain't got no change of drawers, socks, or T-shirts. Get with your girlfriend for me, and tell her I got seven hundred for her to get me four packs of Polo socks, drawers, and T-shirts. Jeff, pass me that paper, cousin," Bay said.

Jeff lifted his pillow up, and there lay the $6,000

in all types of bills, from him and Bay's drawers.

"Boy, fuck her, I got you. This my block; she don't run nothing over here."

"Oh yeah, Shock, get that diesel out then. We running with the boss. Ain't no more middle man, we moving up in the world," Bay smirked.

"Boy, where the fuck y'all get all that from?" she stated as Shock pulled the soul diesel out of the legal envelope with Attorney/Client on it.

"Don't worry about all that. You wanna get this money or not? Because your girlfriend's super ready, and honestly, we ain't got no time as far as wasting."

"Naw, we gonna get this money!"

"Alright, listen, Ciera don't get cut out, okay? She's the one that introduced us to you, and we don't operate like that. It's seven hundred for three of us three packs of sock, drawers and Polo T-shirts. Two thousand for three iPhones, and this little extra three hundred for something good to eat tomorrow, because that shit you served us earlier almost made me think you don't like me," he replied with a smile on his face.

"You're crazy, boy!"

"I'm serious, baby girl. Anyway, that's a even $3,000, $1,500 apiece. Call this number; her name's LaDonna. She gone get the three phones for us. Just tell her what kind we want and that you coming to get them before work tomorrow, alright? We need this ASAP, so make it a priority on your schedule," Bay stated.

"Alright, I got you!"

~ ~ ~

Friday, April 1, 2008

Club Secret was letting out after JB and the mayor just threw their first North Philly all-white-everything party. Coming out of the club were super bad females wearing next to nothing, all leaving in packs of ten, fifteen, and twenty. These bulls really brought the night life to life. All the major players brought their toys out in support and showed love, making the scene look even more on some '86 Paid in Full type shit.

Clark Kent brought his new cocaine-white Rolls

Royce Ghost out. Leaning on the passenger side door was Byrd, dressed in a black lambskin jacket with Chinchilla piped black slacks and Versace loafers. He was talking to a super bad young girl who resembled Rihanna. The mayor was out there in his brand-new Bentley GT, JB was in his Mercedes Benz S-65 AMG, Ab just pulled into the parking lot in his Ferrari, and Champ just pulled up in his all-white hummer throwing hundred dollar bills out the sunroof, with two naked females in the backseat eating each other's pussy. Vito just came through in his Porsche 911, a few other players were out there in Maseratis, and Cumberland Street players came through in two Maybachs and six Escalades.

"Ey, Kent, there goes the lil young bull Keen. I know this little young bull ain't this stupid, bro, he can't be," Byrd stated, looking in the direction of Keen, who was posted outside of a yellow Camaro, talking with three females.

"I got this nigga. I'ma make a movie out this bitch."

"I'm ready, bro! What's the move?"

"Go ahead and pull that joint out of this parking lot," Byrd said as he rolled his ski mask down over his face, then maneuvered through the thick of people still outside the club popping bottles, celebrating and toasting. They were talking shit, spraying champagne all over females and cars. No one noticed Byrd maneuvering low around cars, until he was directly on the other side of Keen's yellow Camaro, Glock 40 in hand.

Also unnoticed was the light-skinned female with red hair, squatting down, giving Keen one of the best dick sucks Byrd ever witnessed. Her girlfriend was also standing around watching her back and enjoying the performance. Still unnoticed, Byrd duck walked right up on Keen, grabbing the back of his neck, and pointed his Glock 40 toward the young female's head.

"Damn, bro, you can't make it this easy. You out here telling people you gonna ride and shit. Fuck you doing, youngin?" Byrd said, patting Keen's waist in search of a pistol. "You out this bitch naked, pants and drawers around your fucking ankles. Naw, lil buddy, keep going, because if you knew better, you'd be out here doing better."

"Please don't kill me," the girl said, scared.

"With one swift motion Byrd removed his gun from the redhead's face and placed it on Keen's forehead."

"Nigga, where the fuck is your car keys, pussy?"

"In my pocket," Keen replied nervously, not knowing the masked man's next move.

"Redhead, get them keys." The little redhead did as she was told, reaching inside Keen's pants pocket and removing his car keys. She also pulled out a large amount of cash. "Lil buddy, that's yours. This ain't no robbery," Byrd stated, taking the car keys from her, then pulling Keen toward the driver's side door. He got inside the driver's seat and pulled Keen's head through the driver's side open window and rolled it all the way up on his neck, leaving only his head inside the car.

"Come on, man, you don't have to do this," he pleaded.

Byrd opened the driver's side door again, put

Keen's car in reverse, and stepped out, leaving Keen semi jogging with the now reversing car.

BOC! BOC! BOC! BOC!

The first four shots ripped through Keen's thigh, ass, and lower back, sending the late-night club goers headed in every direction looking for cover.

BOC! BOC!

The next two shots ripped through his ankle, causing his body to collapse alongside the yellow Camaro door, just in time for impact as his trunk sandwiched the hood of a Buick Park Avenue. Byrd calmly walked toward the passenger side window, checking Keen's slumped body, then walked away like nothing happened.

~ ~ ~

"Yeah, I got with your people last night. She was playing games, so I got y'all some old Boost Mobile phones. That's cool, right?" Boss asked with a smirk on her face, watching Bay's facial expression.

"See, you still thinking you dealing with these regular niggas inside this joint. Once I say do anything out there, it's done, plus they gone find some type of way just to get the message across to me. I already got the message everything was handled. She gave you four thousand from my player, in case we need anything else handled," Bay replied with an even bigger smirk on his face.

RING! RING! RING!

"Boss, A-1-3, alright, alright," she stated into the receiving end of the phone before hanging up and looking Bay straight in his eyes. "Tell your cellmates you have visitors. Go get dressed. I'ma put the socks, drawers, and T-shirts inside your cell now.

"Naw, put theirs inside the cell and bring me a T-shirt and boxers to the shower," Bay stated, then walked off, leaving Boss standing there looking dumb.

Boss sat behind her desk, looked around, then reached into her panties pulling out three duct taped iPhones. She got up and entered the bathroom behind her desk and wrapped the package inside the T-shirt.

"I'll be in the cell," Jeff said, walking off.

CO Boss grabbed the stuff and walked over to a now showering Bay. There was something about these three, because neither her nor Ciera really paid much attention to any other guy or inmate, but already in her mind, there wasn't anything she wouldn't do for Bay.

~~~

On 30th and Allegheny T-Roy sat stationed inside Memo's parking lot, watching as Keisha walked her son into 30th Street Station Barber Shop. As she entered the door, he exited out of his black Camaro dressed in a black and gray Under Armor jogger suit. His hood was already tied extra tight, P95 Ruger thirty-shot clip sticking out of his sweatpants pocket as he crossed 30th Street. Just as he approached the door, he saw Keisha's son being placed inside the barber chair through the window, and proceeded into the shop calm, cool, and collected.

T-Roy walked in the front door and noticed three young bulls already in chairs along with Keisha's son, getting the first little mountain of hair chopped off.

"Damn, bro, y'all in here butchering these kids'
~~~

heads. I've been hearing so much about this shop, and the first thing I see is this," T-Roy said, pointing toward Keisha's son's head.

Just as the barber was about to comment, T-Roy whipped his Ruger out and aimed it toward Keisha's son's head.

"This is how you fade something," T-Roy stated, then fired the first shot.

BOC!

The shot sent the young kid's brains flying all over the wall behind him. Fragments stained the mirror as blood ran down the barber's face. Keisha was frozen in shock, not believing what just took place. She wondered if this was a dream, until reality set in. T-Roy turned his pistol toward her face and fired.

BOC! BOC! BOC! BOC! BOC!

Without missing a beat T-Roy spun his pistol around on everybody in the barber shop, shooting everything and everyone that wasn't nailed down.

~ ~ ~

"Byrd, I wanna come home. I can't stand being

down here no longer. You got me watching these fucking little kids. They keep crying, talking 'bout they want their mom and dad. Stink, I wasn't gone tell you this because I need you focused. Byrd, I'm two months pregnant."

"M, listen, one more month, but until then find us a crib down there. I'm a drive this paper down there this weekend. We ain't coming back up here. I can't trust these niggas," Byrd said, walking around in the Louie store in King Of Prussia Mall with Clark Kent.

"I'm telling you now, Byrd, one month. I can't take this shit no more being alone, missing you. One month or I'm coming back up, and they'll get us dead or alive."

"Alright, alright!" Byrd stated, laughing into the phone knowing Mary was dead serious.

"Babe, I'm not playing, I was two seconds from leaving these kids the other day and coming back up there to be with you. Fuck this, I know your lying. I'm coming now."

"M, don't play with me. One month, end of story."

CHAPTER

14

April 26, 2008

BYRD SAT ON Park Avenue and Allegheny inside his burnt-orange SRT-8 Challenger, going over business with Fatboy, who controlled every major block on that side of Broad Street.

"Damn, bro, I told you it wasn't gone get no sweeter than this."

"Yeah, cousin, them Delaware niggas been coming over the bridge every week for five bricks like clockwork. Plus your man House from Camden, he good for three every four days. Your two blocks, Carlisle and Mayfield Street, doing two bricks a week, and your man Hoc's block doing three bricks a week by itself. Your man Bricks is doing one down Ruby Street every six days. Honestly, cousin, I didn't know your flow was like this," Fatboy told him.

"No bullshit, I ain't do nothing for that flow. That's all my youngins' work! I gotta see to it that them lil niggas touchdown quick, bro. I just screamed at them earlier today, and I gotta handle a few more things. Everything should be back to normal once I finish sweeping the streets. But your good, right?" Byrd asked Fatboy, looking through his Challenger window as T-Roy just pulled up on the other side of the street. He was inside his '87 stealth gray Buick Grand National, with 5 percent tinted windows.

"Yeah, bro, I'm straight! I should be ready for another fifty like next week," Fatboy said.

"Alright, say less! I'ma have Niesha put that together tonight because I might shoot down Atlanta this weekend to go check on a few things I got going on down there," Byrd stated before Fatboy exited the Challenger.

Fatboy pulled off with T-Roy, making a U-turn and following right behind Byrd. He turned left on Park Avenue and Clearfield. Right before getting to 13th Street, he noticed his phone had twenty-five missed calls. Ten was from Niesha, five from Bay, three from Mary, six from his young girl Barbee over in Nice Town, and one from Fatman.

"Bay, what's up with you? Everything good?"

"Yeah, bro, I got everything. Remember that old head Pooh and that shit from the expressway, where homebull got dropped and that news headline had the mask with the quote 'Catch me if you can'? He jumped on that situation, and I got old head handled."

"Hold on, T-Roy right behind me. Let me merge the nigga in," Byrd stated, calling T-Roy's phone on three-way.

"Yo, go 'head, Bay!"

"Yeah, cousin, ol' head all over top of that situation. I got the freak nigga information from the attorney today. His address is 6795 Akaron Street. Plus remember the lil bitch, Felisha, shorty with the star tattooed on her pussy? She jumped on both Green's and ol' head Sharp's case from Broad Street Barber Shop. Ain't really no evidence for nothing else. Shock and Jeff should be getting out tonight. We all had our preliminary hearings today, and they was gonna let them out from CJC (criminal justice center), but they gotta get processed out of state road," Bay said, feeling a little sick his shit wasn't thrown out today.

"Listen, young, I'm on everything tonight. Call your lawyer back and tell him to get you a hearing by next week. Everything should be handled by then. Get that jack out your cell, because once all your witnesses are cleaned up, they coming for you, mark my word. What is the other addresses?"

Bay gave Byrd the addresses for both Felisha and the old head Sharp.

"Alright, we got everything. Get every paper with them folks' names and information out your cell, young. Matter of fact, flush that shit now. I'ma read everything back real quick, double-checking it, then flush it," Byrd stated. He read everything back to Bay, making sure he wrote it down right. Bay confirmed it, then flushed everything down the toilet.

"Alright, listen, tell Shock and Jeff to meet me at the crib on 9th Street off Hunting Park. I'll see you next week, then it will be y'all's turn to clean up my shit, bro."

"Say less, fam," Bay replied.

Two days later Jeff and Shock touched back

down, fully processed out of the system. They had been laying low over at the CO bitch Ciera's crib, waiting on their moment to get back in action. Not being able to get money or touch up on everything Bay needed handled was killing their patience. This very moment they were sitting inside Ciera's living room playing Live basketball on the PlayStation.

"Yo, bro, this waiting around shit's getting on my fucking nerves seriously. On some real shit, I still feel locked up. It doesn't feel any different. I can't move around, and I can't touch no paper."

Just as Shock was telling Jeff what was really going through his mind, Ciera's front window shattered, and what seemed like a fireball came crashing down onto her couch.

"Yo, Shock, throw that shit back out the window," Jeff yelled. "Hurry . . ." Before Jeff finished his statement, all hell broke loose.

BLACCC! BLACCC! BLACCC! BLACC!

"Shock, get that shit out the window," Jeff yelled over the loud explosion of gun fire. He fired wildly out the window, not aiming at anything, just giving

Shock enough time to pick the cocktail up and toss the lit flame back out the window onto the porch.

"Back door, bro, back door," Shock yelled just in time for Jeff to peep the other masked man getting ready to approach the glass door with another Molotov cocktail fire bomb.

"Shoot, shoot, cousin; shoot, nigga." Jeff aimed his .40 caliber pistol toward the back door and let off some quick shots through the back door.

BOC! BOC! BOC! BOC!

Stationed at the end of Ciera's alleyway, sitting in the backseat of a Porsche Cayenne all bandaged up, was Boo. He was waiting for some type of explosion sound, or to see a large fire from the cocktails. The only thing that caught his attention was one young bull limping out of the alley holding his arm, and another dude hauling ass around the corner patting his eyebrows out from the cocktail being thrown back out the window.

"Fuck happened in there? You straight, bull?" Boo asked, pulling his pistol from underneath his leg.

"Naw, I can't fucking see! My eyes, man. Pull

the fuck off. Fuck you still sitting here for? You waiting to go to jail or something?"

"Naw," Boo's other young bull stated, feeling his chest where three bullet holes were as he pulled away from the alley. He thanked God for his bulletproof vest, because without the vest, he would be gone right now.

"Man, what the fuck happened? Wasn't no explosion, only you two niggas coming back around the corner fucked up," Boo stated.

"I don't know!"

"Yo, pull over right there behind that Jag. I'ma get you lil niggas some money. I shouldn't pay y'all shit, but I gotta keep my name clean out here," Boo said, pointing his pistol toward the driver's seat headrest and firing the first shot.

BOC!

"Man, what's up, ol' head?"

BOC! BOC!

Just as the passenger made his statement, two shots were entering his forehead, then flying out the passenger window. Boo threw his hoodie on and exited the backseat, but not before dumping a fresh small bottle of gasoline all over the two dead men's bodies, then striking a match. He jumped inside the Jag, pulling off looking through his rearview mirror. Halfway down the street, the explosion he was looking for brought the night sky to life.

RING!

"Yo?"

"Boo, what's up, what happened? How two niggas you said was gone be dead just call my phone?"

"Ciera, don't call my phone with that stupid-ass shit. Bitch, you told me them niggas would be upstairs. They threw the fucking cocktails back out the window," Boo snapped back, maneuvering the Jag through traffic.

"Alright, you still paying for me to move, right?"

"I know I told you to pack your shit, bitch. I lied." Boo smiled then ended the call, leaving Ciera on the receiving end of a dead call. She shook her head as tears rolled down her face, wondering why she ever crossed Shock and Jeff.

CHAPTER 15

RING! RING!

"Yo, who this?"

"Ey, lil Mark, listen, fish that joint to Bay real quick," Jeff stated. Him and Shock were standing out front of a steak shop on F and Tioga, getting ready to walk across the street to Family Cab.

"Bay!" lil Mark was screaming through the open crack at the bottom of the steel door that separated the door and floor. This was the jailhouse way of communicating crystal clear—getting under the door.

"Yo, bro, listen, I'm ready to send them flicks over from my celly. I know you're over there stressing, bro. I'm sending my line over. You ready?"

"Yeah, go 'head,"

Lil Mark shot the empty milk carton box with the ripped-up sheet attached to it, out from underneath the door. Being a country-seasoned vet at fishing, from 2 cell, his fishing line went right under 9 cell's door.

"Alright, Mark, I got the line. Go 'head and put them flicks on the other end, bro. Then I'm coming right back in your direction with the rest of this food," Bay replied, waiting on the green light from Mark.

"Go 'head, Bay, pull it, bro!"

Bay pulled the fishing line into his cell, put a little fifty ball of sour diesel back on the other end of the line, and told Mark to pull everything back into his cell.

"Yo, what's up?"

"Yo, man, they just blitzed the bitch Ciera's crib. Fuck that shit Byrd talking 'bout 'fall back.' It's on. Then this bitch gone be tripping once she gets home from work, knowing we got into some shit right inside her crib. Man, these niggas tried to cocktail that shit with us inside. Shock threw that shit back out the bitch's window, cousin."

"Hold on, bro? This the bitch Boss right here on the other line," he said as his other line beeped.

"Yo?"

"Listen, Bay, I ain't got shit to do with what Ciera tried to do. I'm not with that shit."

"Boss, what's up? Fuck you talking about?" Bay played dumb in order for Boss to give up the tape.

"Bay, Boo is Ciera's player. From everything I'm getting he was supposed to move her into a new spot. But in order for her to get moved, she had to go against y'all. I never knew you were going to war with Boo, because I would have told you Ciera and Boo was fucking with each other."

"Boss, I'm on the other line with my lawyer. Let me tell him. I'll call right back, hold on. Yo, the bitch Ciera involved in that little hit. That's her and Boo's work. I got a lil dusty bitch named Roz who live right there on 2nd and Cumberland. Hit my jack once you get there. This's her number: 570-999-3100. Tell her you're Bay's brother and to let you chill there for about an hour, alright?" Bay said before clicking back over to Boss. "You still there?"

"Yeah, Bay, that crafty shit ain't inside my blood. Please don't view me in the same light as her; my loyalty is to you. Ciera's mom lives right on Lycoming Avenue inside a bright red house. I'ma call her right now and find out where she's at and give you the address."

"Alright, get with me tomorrow with everything because I can't keep this jack inside my cell. I got too much going on right now, and I can't jeopardize my freedom, dig me? so make sure you got all the necessary information once you come into work tomorrow, alright?" Bay stated, ending the call.

Ten minutes later, he redialed Jeff's number. "Yo, you get there yet?"

"Yeah, we just walked through shorty's door. Damn, Bay, shorty super thick. Fuck you been hiding her at?"

"Man, fuck her right now. Call Byrd's number. Naw, listen, tell Roz to get that duffle bag out the basement for y'all. Matter of fact, put her on the phone," Bay stated.

"What's up, Bay?"

"What's up, baby girl, you straight out there? Listen, get everything together for my folks 'cause they gone need it, plus tell your little brother I need that favor now. Ride with them and bring his lil Rican homies out the cut. You got me, right?" Bay asked.

"You already know, papi."

"That's my girl."

That night was the beginning of another operation. Bay kept the phone for another two hours calling a few different numbers. He got with Bricks from down Ruby Street and told him about the situation at hand, and to his surprise his man was fucking lil Felisha a.k.a. Star. They merged his man Joey in from OT, who was moving perk thirties out the Northeast heavy. To Bricks's and Bay's surprise, Kenny was cellmates with Joey's man Bam from West Philly. He was awaiting trial for a double homicide.

After about forty-five minutes of conversation, the party of three agreed upon giving Bam's brother two bricks and $4,000 for the hit on Kenny's life inside his cell. Bricks would get his man to bring Felisha down Ruby Street, and she'd be handled down there with great attention for her role in falsifying a statement against a good nigga. The only thing that was left on the table now was Sharp. Bay just finished speaking with Jeff about putting Roz's little brother's crew on.

Once he finished tightening those few loose ends up, Bay chopped it up with Trina, who he was supposed to get with. She sent a few pictures to the phone, fueling Bay's fire, making him want to fuck her even more, but the picture that took the cake was her swinging from a sex swing over her bed with a lime-green dildo shoved inside her pussy. Bay damn near lost his mind once that image shot across his iPhone screen. Without thinking twice, that became his screensaver.

"Ey, Mark, you up, bro? Tell your celly them flicks super nutty, bro. I'm about to send some super heavy work over there, cousin. Send me that line over, y'all tripping over there. That's the type of work that be coming up on Tuesday and Thursday. Oh man, y'all going out with me this Friday?" Bay asked.

He wrapped his iPhone inside the shirt, waiting for Mark to shoot the fishing line back across. Bay really took a liking to Mark and his celly. They were the only two allowed to use his phone, which he had put a $100 on.

CHAPTER 16

"WHEN I WALK up in this bitch, they turn the lights out, all these young niggas with me and they iced out. I had to stack it up and get my mom a nice house, I could of did the wrath, but I brought the bikes out. Yeah we never live for tomorrow, new half-a-brick in a car, rich and my chick is a star, I never wished on a star."

"Kenny, man, turn that shit down, bro. I'm trying to pay attention. Make sure these fucking cops ain't walking down the tiers. Only thing you wanna do is smoke and fucking joke. This ain't no fucking game, bro, this is jail. You gotta stop playing so much. Look, they running up inside Tay and them's cell now. Look at that shit, bro, and you playing games."

Kenny's rat ass hopped down off the top bunk, nervous, sliding his shower shoes on and coming to the door where Bam was peeking through the towel that was hanging over the small plexiglass window.

"Nigga, move so I can see what the fuck you

talking about. You standing right here blocking the view," Kenny stated as Bam maneuvered himself out of the way. He gave Kenny a full view of what wasn't going on outside the cell, blinding him from paying attention to what was getting ready to happen inside the cell.

"Pussy, you rat-ass nigga," Bam stated as he brought the knife down in Kenny's neck with full force.

"CO, help, help, cell 26," Kenny yelled out, trying to hit the call button and fight off the attack that was taking place. Bam repeatedly forced the knife into his back, neck, and head.

"Shut the fuck up, you rat-ass nigga. You out here telling on good niggas, pussy. You gone die today." Bam forced his knife in Kenny's head. "This is why real niggas can't do epic shit, 'cause you rat-ass niggas scared of the dark. Y'all all want the light, pussy. Well reach for the light; God's calling you now, nigga," Bam stated, still stabbing Kenny repeatedly, over more than two hundred times.

After repeatedly stabbing Kenny's lifeless body,

blood was everywhere inside the small cell. The floor, ceiling, sink, and toilet were now a crimson red. Bam pulled Kenny's empty commissary box from underneath their bunk. He emptied the gray bin, which contained a few soups, two tunas, and two bags of hot chips, onto his bunk, then folded Kenny's body up and stuffed his rat ass inside the box.

Twenty minutes later, cell 26 was spotless. Bam bird bathed himself then walked toward the door. He hit the call button and came out carrying him and Kenny's che-che bag headed to the 190-degree hot water sink for water. Bam acted as if nothing took place inside his cell a few minutes ago.

"Sherrel, listen, I need some cleaning products. My stupid ass celly fucked my whole cell up and gone leave this nasty-ass smell inside that joint."

"Go 'head, Bam. Everything is right there. Make sure you return my shit, and don't use up everything either. I ain't playing."

"Ain't nobody gone use all your funky-ass supplies," Bam smiled, going under the cabinet grabbing the bleach, Pine-Sol, and a few other things and then heading back to his cell. Once back inside his cell, he poured the 190-degree hot water inside the commissary bin over Kenny's body. Then he dumped a fresh bottle of baby oil inside with the bleach to mix with the rest of the mixture of products. Bam watched as Kenny's skin melted off the bone right before his very eyes.

"Damn, nigga, they say two wrongs don't make it right, but if it's my blood then someone's got to die, and a rat's life ain't worth more than no real one," Bam stated, lifting the commissary box over the toilet and pouring the mixture inside the toilet before repeating the process and pouring it out once again.

Taking Kenny's body out of the commissary box and placing the head up against the toilet, he began stumping it right off his shoulders until it separated from his body. He repeated the process with his arms and legs.

~ ~ ~

Around 7:30 a.m. the very next morning, Byrd was up earlier than normal, stationed a few doors down from the ol' head Sharp's crib on E. Plymouth Street. From watching his every move, the past few days, Byrd learned that he walked his dog every morning between 7:15 and 7:25 a.m. and was back inside his house by 7:30. Today was different though because there was light rain outside, which was perfect being that it was May 1, 2008. The saying was wrong about April showers bringing May flowers. On this very day, light rain caused it to be misty out, which meant Sharp wasn't coming out.

Byrd decided he was going in. He fished around in his backseat searching for his black Champion hoodie and ski mask. Once he threw his pullover hoodie over his head and pulled his ski mask down over his face, Byrd exited his Silverado pickup truck. He noticed a Comcast Cable truck parked in front of 4619 E Plymouth.

"Man, what the fuck? This can't be happening. On all the days, this nigga wanna fix some fucking cable today," Byrd said out loud as he watched the two Comcast workers get out of their truck and approach Sharp's door with tools in hand.

Byrd decided to wait a few minutes and then operate on both the workers and Sharp. As these thoughts were running through his head, Byrd watched the young Puerto Rican male ring Sharp's door bell, while his co-worker wrote something down on his clipboard. Seconds later Sharp answered the door. Byrd could see the party of three exchanging words. He saw Sharp's puzzled facial expression and knew something wasn't right, but he wasn't moving until his job was complete. At that very moment, Byrd noticed the young Rican standing on the left go inside his tool box and withdraw the biggest .44 Magnum handgun he had ever seen. As quick as the Comcast worker pulled it out, Sharp's brains stained his glass door and floor behind him.

"Goddamn, this nigga fucking crazy," Byrd stated. He watched as the Rican stood over him, hitting him three more times.

Sliding lower in his driver's seat, below the steering wheel, he reached inside his center console retrieving his iPhone.

"Answer the phone, cousin, damn," Byrd said to himself as he waited for Jeff to answer.

He crawled between the space separating the passenger and driver's seat, then pulled the left back seat down and crawled inside.

"Yo, bro," Byrd stated as Jeff answered, whispering into the receiving. "Listen, cousin, I'm right here on Sharp's block. Man, two Rican young bulls just did Sharp dirty, cousin. You're not gonna believe my fucking luck. I'm stuck a few doors down from homebull's crib. You gotta get somebody to come drive the Silverado off this block, bro."

"Alright, say less, bro. What's the address, cousin?" Jeff stated, rolling out of Shakeya's bed, leaving her naked ass in plain sight for whomever to witness as he jumped out of the bed dialing Cookie's number on three-way.

"Cookie, I need a little favor. Byrd, what's the address, cousin?" Jeff asked, listening to him repeat the address. "Alright, go get him. Byrd, lock her number inside your phone. Tell him the number, Cook!"

"I'm locking it in now," Byrd replied.

"Alright, I'm ready to get with Shock. Get with me tonight, bro," Jeff said, sliding his other Prada sneaker on. He crept out of Keya's house and jumped into his Chrysler 300.

~ ~ ~

"Shake down, shake down! Here they come. The water's off and turtles are on the move. They're coming suited and booted through the sally port and fire escape."

Everybody with a full view of the sally port and fire escape started yelling, trying to alert the rest of A-1-3.

"Pop cell 9," one of three search team officers yelled out, standing along with US Marshals, the head district attorney Lynne Abraham, and four homicide agents.

"Bay Davis, turn around and put your hands above your head, please," the US Marshall stated, retrieving a set of handcuffs.

"Man, you must be fucking kidding me. I ain't putting my fucking hands above my head so you can fucking kill me inside this cell," Bay stated, backing toward the bunks inside his cell, hoping and praying this big-ass incredible hawk agent didn't come into the cell on no dumb shit.

"Listen, you got five seconds before we come inside that cell and destroy your little ass. Now, what's it gonna be?" the incredible hawk lookalike asked.

He started strapping his gloves on super tight hoping Bay would refuse. He thought about the circumstances of the situations and knew better. Wasn't nothing inside his cell, no mail, no phone, nothing!

"Alright, listen, I'm putting my fucking hands up. Ain't nothing wrong with me physically or mentally. Don't twist my wrist, and don't try breaking my arm or none of that shit. I ain't answering no questions until my lawyer is present, so come on," Bay stated, allowing the agents to place the handcuffs around his wrists.

They escorted him out of the cell, and the rest of the pod went crazy screaming and throwing all types of shit out of their cells. Bay looked toward Lynne Abraham and smirked.

"This the trouble you wanna go up against? It's a no-win battle, because fucking with me means you're fucking with them. We all animals living inside this crazy jungle. You thought you had control over us. This ain't office mat. You can't walk inside here and demand shit. Look around, remember these faces, because they'll remember yours. When we sleep at night it's your face we see. A good friend once told me, 'Study the board and remember the players that's gunning for you.' I would never forget you, so I'm glad you exposed your identity. I'm grateful for that gesture of kindness, and I appreciate that. Look around, and pay good attention to that sound. You hear it? Now welcome to the fucking jungle," Bay boasted, hog spitting at Lynne Abraham's feet. That gesture gave the whole housing unit fuel for an already burning fire.

They started banging on the doors with commissary boxes and any other item that was inside their cells. The whole top tier flooded their cells, causing toilet water to run like a river down the stairs and over the tier. A few inmates lit fires and fished the flaming balls under their doors, causing marshals and corrections officers to get behind the special turtle unit. Lynne Abraham stood there frustrated and pissed off over the power struggle, which she was losing. The inmates were going ape shit in the housing unit.

Bay stood in the sally port witnessing the power and hunger inside these inmates, and knew once his situation turned in a different direction, this would be the control and leadership that was necessary. It wasn't about the cars or money; it was about loyalty to a cause, the right cause. Freedom from oppression and democracy, pledge World Gang or nothing else.

"Miss, allow me to show you what power is when leadership is in the right hands. You leaving me here inside this sally port is gonna start a riot. These young niggas' respect is real, and you and your goon squad are looking familiar," Bay stated through the cracked door, smiling on the other end.

"Alright, let him back on the pod," the lead white

shirt stated, overriding, and not giving a fuck about anybody else's concern as long as his staff got control back over this housing unit. Bay strolled back down toward his cell holding a closed fist in the air, as if to make a statement on a new movement.

"Pledge World Gang! It's no other show on earth that's greater," Bay shouted, walking back into a flipped-upside-down cell. Lynne Abraham looked toward the white shirt.

"Once this block is back under the control of your officers, lock that inmate in solitary confinement for the remainder of his stay here. There's no way one man should have all that power. I'll be damned if I'm made a fool of again. Am I clear?"

"Yes ma'am!"

CHAPTER 17

"BEGINNING OF FIRST forty-eight hours! The streets is not only watchin' but they talkin' now? Shit they got me circlin' the block before I'm parkin now."

"Damn, bro, you got me holding on to these joints. If you ain't heavy as my folks stated, speak on it. That way we can maneuver around all the bullshit and I can get you on a much heavier level. If you gone be in bed with my lil cousin, I gotta make sure she secure on all levels," Det. Gram said, looking over toward his female partner, who played the roll of his cousin. She met Boo on South Street inside the Adidas store.

"Listen, bro, you talking peanut to an elephant. Right now my plate's been a little full, but since you speaking upon givin' this help that's needed to me, make the order at fifteen flat and sixteen for the other hundred you fronting me, and we could get the ball rolling right now. I ride around with two tickets (million) on me at all times, lightweight emergency contact money, and I'm dialing your number right now. Do you accept this call, or you pump faking?" Boo asked, already making his mind up that he was running off on this plug.

"You ain't saying nothing slick to a can of oil. Where we meeting at?" Det. Gram replied, recording every word Boo said into his electronic device that was stationed on his steering wheel.

"Blockbuster, right there off Hunting Park. It's 10:30 a.m. now, 3:00 p.m. sharp, I wait for no man. A second too long could be life or death. On time always mean success, dig me!"

"Got you, bro," Det. Gram replied, smiling from ear to ear, knowing this was a major bust for him and his partner.

Boo ended the phone call and looked across toward his young bull's face, who was riding shotgun inside his Ram 1500 pickup truck.

"Nigga, you ready? This is two hundred free bricks. I'm trying to make you the first young sixteen-year-old millionaire. All you gotta do is do what you do best."

"What's that?" he asked curiously.

"Kill shit little niggas," Boo stated, fueling shorty's already burning hunger.

"I'm ready, bro!"

~ ~ ~

"Goddamn every fucking time we get some type of break in this fucking case or any case that pertains to these fucking animals, our witnesses end up dead or missing in fucking action," Det. Link stated, knocking a full stack of paperwork clear off his desk.

"Link, you gotta be patient, and stop taking your fucking work home with you. These cases are becoming more personal for you. Remember, it's just work! It's our job to catch these monsters, not become one," Det. Samsung explained, picking up the stack of paperwork off the marble floor and placing it back on the already messy desk inside homicide headquarters.

"Sam, you don't understand. They went up to that jail three days ago, fucking with this kid, letting him know we didn't have no evidence on him. Today my fucking phone is ringing off the fucking hook. James Scott, the guy Pooh, was found dead this morning at 5:45 a.m. on Broad and Lehigh Avenue, under the Amtrak train station. Sam, this fucking guy's body was found on the tracks. His head was separated from his body. They identified the guy by his fucking fingerprints. The fucking train's actual wheel had his eyeball smashed and wrapped up around its breaks. Then homicide received a call this morning telling us that a female's body was found inside a fucking lion's den inside the Philadelphia Zoo. We get there thinking maybe a zookeeper slipped over into the den, but instead, it's this young animal's other fucking witness, the female, Felisha White, with a dead rat shoved down her throat. We sent a radio call across the scanner. Anybody inside the area of E. Plymouth, the 4600 block, get to 4619 quickly and survey the area. Sam, they got there and the man was already lying inside his doorway with a bullet hole in his head."

"Damn, that's crazy!"

"Yeah, and on top of that, a dog was licking his

face. These fucking guys are monsters, and it's clear that we're not dealing with the average group of punks. These are serious killers, who are willing and able to murder at the drop of a hat for each other," Det. Link stated, frustrated and burnt out.

RING! RING!

"Yes, Link speaking," he answered. "You can't be fucking serious. This is every fucking witness within twenty-four hours. Alright, me and my partner will be there in twenty minutes. I guess I'll be taking my work home again with me, because that was a call from the correction institution CFCF. Our confidential informant Kenneth Ruff was just found on a different housing block dead and stuffed inside a commissary bin with every bone separated from his body." Det. Link's partner shook his head in disbelief.

~ ~ ~

It was 2:30 p.m., and Boo was already sitting in the parking lot of Blockbuster on Broad and Hunting Park. He drove by a few different spots seeing what was perfect for his young bull Face to be stationed at.

Upon observing the lot, he decided on having Face positioned to make a clean getaway to Roosevelt Boulevard, in case things didn't go right.

"Face Mob, you ready, bro? It's going down in a few minutes, bro. You ready to be a fucking millionaire, nigga? We talking extra cheese on everything, bro, no more struggling. I'm talking about ready-made millions, young rich nation, nigga," Boo stated into the receiving end of his phone, hyping his young bull up. He stared out the front window of his Ford Mustang GT.

"Bro, I've been waiting on this moment my whole life, folk. I swear, bro, you won't regret putting me on this type of lick. Not only will I forever be loyal, but, bro, I'm a murder. Anything that get in your way, bro," Face replied from the driver's seat of his Nissan GTR.

"That's what the fuck I like to hear, lil nigga!"

Stationed all around Blockbuster were different tactical teams. Right there on Hunting Park at the bus stop was Agent Mark, armed and ready. Agent Gram and his partner sat across the street on Broad Street waiting a few more seconds before pulling over into the parking lot. Det. Williams and his partner were undercover Blockbuster employees behind the counter. They were waiting for their moment to engage in the operation that would soon be taking place outside the video store. Agent James Harris and his partner were stationed inside a GameStop truck.

"Here goes everything," Det. Gram stated to his female partner as they pulled into the parking lot inside their Silverado pickup truck.

"Make the call, Gram, and tell him it's 2:55. Let him know we're on his time. Late means we leave, because I don't see his car," Det. Brown said.

"Yo?"

"We're here! This ain't that type of spot to be waiting around. Plus I got other shit I gotta handle, so timing is everything, bro."

"No doubt. I'm right around the corner about to pull into the lot now. It just turned 3:00, bro. What car y'all in?"

"Dark blue Silverado. How are we gonna play this situation out? You want me and Jazz to jump out and switch cars with you?" Det. Gram asked, still recording every moment of their conversation through his electronic communication device. As Boo surveilled the parking lot from across the street, he spotted the Silverado truck pulling into an open parking spot, and texted Face's phone from his other iPhone.

"Dark blue Silverado, green light."

"That's cool; we can just switch wheels. I'm right here inside the Camry. Listen, the paper is inside the trunk. I'm putting it in the backseat now," Boo stated, watching someone he didn't even know go inside the Camry trunk. The guy placed a few bags inside their backseat and walked toward the GameStop.

"Alright, me and Jazz gone leave the truck running for you. Hit my phone once you're in a safe zone."

"What about the stuff?"

"Just hit the defrost button, hold the brake, and tap your turn signal down. The whole back cab mouth gonna open, and all two hundred will be waiting for you."

Detectives Gram and Brown exited their vehicle and headed toward the Camry, when they noticed a young kid getting ready to jump inside their Silverado. Just as Face was getting ready to grab the door handle, Det. Gram spun into action, rushing back in the direction of the pickup truck. He was thinking that this couldn't be his luck, a fucking kid playing around with the biggest bust of his fucking career by trying to steal a fucking car.

"Kid get the fuck away from that car, shit head. This ain't no fucking game," Gram shouted, as he walked toward the kid.

As Gram approached Face, Face spun around clutching a chrome and black Smith & Wesson handgun, aiming directly at Det. Gram's face.

"Pussy, keep walking toward me. Don't make no sudden moves. I swear, any wrong moves and you're gonna die today. Do as I say, and you'll leave this parking lot with your life," Face said, walking toward Det. Gram. He wrapped his arm over Gram's shoulders and stuck his gun into his gut while escorting him to the passenger side door.

"Listen, kid, you really don't wanna do this. I'm telling you now this type of trouble is out of your league. Whoever put you up to this sent you on a crash course to hell. If you continue on with this, I won't be able to help you."

"Pussy, get the fuck inside the wheel; less talking and more action. Now move over and complete that process and show me those joints, nigga," Face said, feeling the excitement as Det. Gram moved over and did as he was told.

Once he finished performing the special sequence, the entire backseat folded up, sliding into the floor. It exposed a nineteen-by-twenty-inch hole. Then a few seconds later the bed of the cab lifted showing what seemed to be two hundred white powdered bricks of cocaine.

"Damn, nigga, if my old head didn't think you was super nutty, I would have let your bitch ass live!" Soon as Face made that statement Det. Gram made his move.

He swiftly punched Face across the jaw and jumped out of the driver's side door with lightning speed. Face shook the blow off and jumped into the driver's seat firing wildly out the driver's side window. He was going against everything Boo told him to do. All the other detectives that were in on the sting came to their colleague's rescue, firing wildly at the speeding Silverado exiting out of the parking lot heading toward Roosevelt Boulevard.

"All units take the kid alive. I repeat, alive. That's not our man. The kid is around sixteen or seventeen years old, black male, short dark hair, no facial hair, black Dickies suit. He's armed and dangerous. If possible take the kid alive," Det. Brown stated as she and Det. Gram jumped inside the GameStop work truck that was parked in the lot.

All the agents rushed to their squad cars and jumped into the pursuit. They chased Face down Roosevelt Boulevard, with Boo still watching from across the street, shaking his head as he witnessed his soldier make a critical mistake by shooting in the first place. Now knowing Jazz and her folks wasn't street people, but federal agents, he knew shit really had taken a turn for the worst, and Face didn't even know he was knee deep up Shit Creek without a paddle. Then he thought about the conversations he had with the agent over the phone and banged his head up against the steering wheel before pulling out of the parking spot following the last agent that entered her car.

Face maneuvered the Silverado through traffic, in and out of different lanes while dialing Shock's number on his cell phone. He noticed the sea of unmarked cars through his rearview mirror, and did a double check making sure his eyes were seeing correctly.

"Yo, Shock, listen, man, I got the fucking work, but you ain't gone fucking believe this shit, bro."

"What's happening?"

"The fucking cops or feds are all over me right now. I took the whole load and wheel, bro."

"Where are you now?"

"I just passed Front and the Boulevard. I'm about to come back around, so be ready, bro, please," Face stated, pushing the end button and busting a wild U-turn, causing a major five-car crash.

He then maneuvered through the small open space, panicking, and not paying full attention to the road. Just as he squeezed through the opening, a man selling ice-cold waters was just backing away from a paying customer. Face made impact with the water man's body at a very high rate of speed, causing the older guy to fly up into the air upon impact.

The man came back down headfirst, smashing his skull upon impact with the concrete. Face witnessed the man landing through his rearview mirror and became more scared. Still in panic mode, he forced the Silverado up the back of another car, using that vehicle to ram another vehicle, and maneuvered his way throughout traffic. He shot across the Boulevard into oncoming traffic, causing another massive accident. This time it was a ten-car crash.

Just as Face made it back to 9th and Roosevelt Boulevard, he shot across the four-lane highway. Panic and fear exited his body as he saw Shock and damn near forty young niggas on dirt bikes and four-wheelers directing traffic, making a clear path for him to drive through, like they were parting the Red Sea and he was that messenger from the man above with two hundred reasons why they were a few seconds from going ape shit. Soon as he made his way through the sea of motorbikes, Shock shot into action, taking off at a very high rate of speed, leaving the rest of his crew members to begin purging on what seemed like a few hundred police and other agents.

BLACCC! BLACCC! BLACCC! BOC! BOC! BOC! BOOM! BOOM!

The barrage of bullets had civilians ducking and dodging, trying to find a safe area for them to hide. The whole scene was spiraling out of control.

Throughout everything that was taking place, Agent Gram was thinking about being played by Boo and wanted revenge. He was going to stop at nothing to lay that motherfucker down. The whole time he was mad at himself, the person he wanted revenge on was looking on from a few feet away plotting his own revenge as he watched Face make a getaway.

CHAPTER 18

"YOUR BODY IS my playground, let me lick you up and down, make you feel like a woman should, it seems like you ready, seems like you ready, to go all the way . . ."

A few miles away and a few hours later Byrd was relaxing in his penthouse hotel suite, with lit candles lined up across the hardwood floor. Red rose petals shaped like an arrow pointed toward another section, followed by more rose petals and candles leading toward the master bathroom where candles surrounded the huge master tub. A gold bottle of Ace of Spade sat on the floor on top of a tray with strawberries and whipped cream. The tub seemed as if it was gonna overflow with bubbles from the bubble bath. R. Kelly set the tone for the type of night it was gonna be.

RING!

"Hello?"

"Mr. Bond, you have a Mrs. Bond here waiting

to be escorted up to the penthouse if you wish to accept her entry to the top floor."

"Yes, but she needs no escort. I'll be waiting at the door. Matter fact, just tell her PH 15c."

"Okay, sir, she's on her way up. If you need anything else just call down and ask for Jack."

"Will do, sir, but I assure you she's all I need tonight," Byrd replied, thinking about the last time him and Mary had been in each other's company.

Byrd's one-month mark had come and gone. Mary told Byrd it wasn't up for debate, and she was on her way back to Philly. They went back and forth for an hour before Mary said she was about two hours away. That made Byrd smile knowing how hardheaded she was, and he rushed around trying to find a penthouse for them before going back down to Atlanta, Georgia, with her. Everything was already cleaned up with Bay. His attorney already stated he should be out within seventy-two hours due to his Rule 600 petition. Lynne Abraham announced on television she didn't have enough evidence on anybody inside the World Gang circle. Byrd stood there accepting her apology.

When Mary entered the penthouse door, there was no hesitation. She kissed Byrd then removed her trench coat, exposing her naked body to the warmth of Byrd's tongue. He slid his tongue and hands around her nipples and down toward her naval, placing a light kiss right above her clean, freshly Brazilian waxed pussy. He then stuck his hands between her legs, spreading them apart, lifting Mary's five-foot-two-inch frame on top of his shoulders, carrying her now trembling body toward the master bathroom, never missing one beat from removing his tongue from Mary's pussy. She tightly wrapped her legs around Byrd's neck, craving for his touch, praying this moment wouldn't stop. She instantly exploded into his mouth. Cum ran down his chin, tasting so good to him that he almost forgot this was only the beginning stages of tonight.

Before it was said and done, he planned on exploring every corner, crack, and cut of her body, along with strawberries and a few glasses of Ace of Spade.

"Oh my God, Byrd, please don't stop, pleasssse don't stop, babe. Ooh, I miss you so fuuuucking much. Pleasssse, please don't stop! Can I cum again, please let me cuuuuum, oooh my God," Mary yelled out, not giving a flying fuck who could hear her, as long as he didn't stop.

Byrd finished teasing her body and placed her inside the warm bubble bath tub, then proceeded to fill two glasses with the Ace of Spade and feed Mary her first strawberry dipped in chocolate.

"Damn, you really miss me, huh? I hope you ready for tonight, and are able to keep up," Byrd said, looking Mary directly in her green eyes while light tears rolled into the tub off her beautiful face.

"Yes, I'm ready. Can we skip this and go straight to the bedroom? I want you inside me right now."

"Be patient, the night is still young, stink. We gotta few toasts to make: new baby, happy life, happy wife, right? So, let's live in the moment, alright? Don't you worry about anything. I got us!" He gently kissed her tears off her face.

~ ~ ~

"Byrd, they coming, they coming, bro. Wake up, it's going down, bro!"

Unaware of his own surroundings, Byrd really didn't recognize anything that was coming out of Loon's mouth, until he heard the loud sound from the steel ram going up against the front door. He then realized Mary wasn't in sight and that the reason for his own face being wet was from his dog, Killer, licking all over his mouth and face.

"Police, police, search warrant, get down, everybody get down . . . upstairs."

BOOM! The back door came crashing in.

"Police, police, search warrant," the second team was screaming as they broke down the back door and rushed through the kitchen. Both tactical teams, fully engaged, locked and loaded, ransacked every corner of Loon's aunt Sue's house.

"Black male on the move. We got action upstairs."

"Movement, movement," another officer started yelling as he and Byrd locked eyes. Byrd made his exit toward the back room window.

“Freeze, muthafucker. Don’t move, he gotta gun.”

“GUN! GUN! GUN!” the tactical team officer started yelling. Without hesitation, the tactical team officer fired off his first shot in Byrd’s direction

BUC.

The single shot ripped through Byrd, sending him crashing through the back room window, causing everyone in the household to go ape shit. Out of nowhere, Killer came charging from the middle room, down the stairs, barking and jumping straight for the first tactical squad officer’s throat.

BOOM!

“He shot the fucking dog,” Sue started yelling, trying to shake free of the hand of a female officer who was pinning her down on the floor.

As the first shot went off, Loon’s aunt came rushing into her kitchen raising hell, throwing pots and pans, cursing, exposing her naked ass and flashing brown hard nipples through her night gown.

Loon just sat quietly, praying and hoping Byrd was still alive as he watched what he assumed to be a dead friend lying on his aunt's back porch.

"Man, this shit ain't necessary. Y'all fucking ain't got no warrant for this. We know our rights. Where's the search warrant? Let us see what type warrant was issued, because if it's a body warrant and y'all fuck this house up we suing the shit out of this city," Loon's uncle Big stated from the living room floor, handcuffed and violated.

Once the house was clear and they found no sign of drugs being inside, agent Adam Morgan knew this wasn't going to end well, because the warrant they were issued was only a body warrant and the man lying on the floor was right: he now knew they were up Shit Creek without paddles this time around.

Outside, sitting in a dark Ford Explorer, was little Reese's mother, Janet, still up to her old tricks, try'na find ways to make a dishonest buck and use the lives of those who helped her family survive for years.

Meanwhile

Across the street being nosey was Shay sticking

her head out the window try'na be the first neighborhood reporter to break everything down, only to see Reese's mom smoking a cigarette through the cracked window, sitting beside another agent getting live play-by-play action over his walkie-talkie, shaking his head in disbelief that Janet's information didn't produce Byrd and the amount of drugs on a silver platter as promised.

As both tactical teams made their exit, Sue's block was full of onlookers as her front door lay on her living room floor.

"What the fuck is all y'all motherfuckers standing around being nosey for? Act like y'all ain't never see motherfuckers run up in somebody's house for no reason. What y'all should be doing is recording this shit," Sue said, standing in her doorway with her exposed nipples hanging out, pointing toward her front door.

"Somebody gonna pay for this shit: police brutality, sexual harassment, destroying property. Oh yeah, we got everything on these motherfuckers. I bet they'll think twice before they run up inside the next black person's crib. Got me coming out here with my titties out, not respecting my privacy."

By now a few people had their camera phones out recording everything Sue was saying. A few even felt sorry for her and started chanting "BLACK LIVES MATTER!" and "FUCK THE POLICE!"

"That's fucking right. Don't let these motherfuckers come in our neighborhood and tear our shit up. My house is y'all's fucking house. Fuck these pigs," Sue yelled, spitting directly in the face of one of the officers and giving him a look as if to say, "Do something."

"At that very moment, Byrd was being carried out by two officers, who tossed his limp body into the backseat of their squad car. His eye's continued to roll back and forth as he felt more and more like he was heading toward the end of the road."

"Pour out a little liquor, Bury me in some Evisu jeans. A USDA top and a throw-away Glock. Bury me a G, nothin' more nothin' less. When I get where I'm goin', I just gotta be fresh. Expect the worst, but hope for the best. But you know how it is, amen God bless. I can't leave now niggas owe me money. My nigga on the westside owe me 'bout a dub. And my partner with a few, shit he owe a nigga too. I should'a hugged my son, should'a kissed my mother. Spent some time with her, show her I love her. Every night she was prayin' for me, I was in the streets . . . Pour out a little liquor, bury me a G."

Young Jeezy's song played in Byrd's head. As his thoughts continued, he drifted further away from the light . . .

Text Good2Go at 31996 to receive new release updates via text message.

To order books, please fill out the order form below:

To order films please go to ***www.good2gofilms.com***

Name:____

Address:____

City: _____________ State: ______ Zip Code: ____________________

Phone:____

Email:____

Method of Payment: Check VISA MASTERCARD

Credit Card#:____

Name as it appears on card: ____________________________

Signature: ____

Item Name	Price	Qty	Amount
48 Hours to Die – Silk White	$14.99		
A Hustler's Dream - Ernest Morris	$14.99		
A Hustler's Dream 2 - Ernest Morris	$14.99		
Bloody Mayhem Down South	$14.99		
Business Is Business – Silk White	$14.99		
Business Is Business 2 – Silk White	$14.99		
Business Is Business 3 – Silk White	$14.99		
Childhood Sweethearts – Jacob Spears	$14.99		
Childhood Sweethearts 2 – Jacob Spears	$14.99		
Childhood Sweethearts 3 - Jacob Spears	$14.99		
Childhood Sweethearts 4 - Jacob Spears	$14.99		
Connected To The Plug – Dwan Marquis Williams	$14.99		
Connected To The Plug 2 – Dwan Marquis Williams	$14.99		
Deadly Reunion – Ernest Morris	$14.99		
Flipping Numbers – Ernest Morris	$14.99		
Flipping Numbers 2 – Ernest Morris	$14.99		
He Loves Me, He Loves You Not - Mychea	$14.99		
He Loves Me, He Loves You Not 2 - Mychea	$14.99		
He Loves Me, He Loves You Not 3 - Mychea	$14.99		
He Loves Me, He Loves You Not 4 – Mychea	$14.99		
He Loves Me, He Loves You Not 5 – Mychea	$14.99		
Lord of My Land – Jay Morrison	$14.99		
Lost and Turned Out – Ernest Morris	$14.99		
Married To Da Streets – Silk White	$14.99		
M.E.R.C. - Make Every Rep Count Health and Fitness	$14.99		
Money Make Me Cum – Ernest Morris	$14.99		
My Besties – Asia Hill	$14.99		

My Besties 2 – Asia Hill	$14.99		
My Besties 3 – Asia Hill	$14.99		
My Besties 4 – Asia Hill	$14.99		
My Boyfriend's Wife - Mychea	$14.99		
My Boyfriend's Wife 2 – Mychea	$14.99		
My Brothers Envy – J. L. Rose	$14.99		
My Brothers Envy 2 – J. L. Rose	$14.99		
Naughty Housewives – Ernest Morris	$14.99		
Naughty Housewives 2 – Ernest Morris	$14.99		
Naughty Housewives 3 – Ernest Morris	$14.99		
Naughty Housewives 4 – Ernest Morris	$14.99		
Never Be The Same – Silk White	$14.99		
Stranded – Silk White	$14.99		
Slumped – Jason Brent	$14.99		
Supreme & Justice – Ernest Morris	$14.99		
Tears of a Hustler - Silk White	$14.99		
Tears of a Hustler 2 - Silk White	$14.99		
Tears of a Hustler 3 - Silk White	$14.99		
Tears of a Hustler 4- Silk White	$14.99		
Tears of a Hustler 5 – Silk White	$14.99		
Tears of a Hustler 6 – Silk White	$14.99		
The Panty Ripper - Reality Way	$14.99		
The Panty Ripper 3 – Reality Way	$14.99		
The Solution – Jay Morrison	$14.99		
The Teflon Queen – Silk White	$14.99		
The Teflon Queen 2 – Silk White	$14.99		
The Teflon Queen 3 – Silk White	$14.99		
The Teflon Queen 4 – Silk White	$14.99		
The Teflon Queen 5 – Silk White	$14.99		
The Teflon Queen 6 - Silk White	$14.99		
The Vacation – Silk White	$14.99		
Tied To A Boss - J.L. Rose	$14.99		
Tied To A Boss 2 - J.L. Rose	$14.99		
Tied To A Boss 3 - J.L. Rose	$14.99		

Tied To A Boss 4 - J.L. Rose	$14.99		
Tied To A Boss 5 - J.L. Rose	$14.99		
Time Is Money - Silk White	$14.99		
Two Mask One Heart – Jacob Spears and Trayvon Jackson	$14.99		
Two Mask One Heart 2 – Jacob Spears and Trayvon Jackson	$14.99		
Two Mask One Heart 3 – Jacob Spears and Trayvon Jackson	$14.99		
Wrong Place Wrong Time – Silk White	$14.99		
Young Goonz – Reality Way	$14.99		
Subtotal:			
Tax:			
Shipping (Free) U.S. Media Mail:			
Total:			

Make Checks Payable To:
Good2Go Publishing
7311 W Glass Lane,
Laveen, AZ 85339